A FINE DAY FOR MURDER

LEXIE CARVER

A Fine Day for Murder

by Lexie Carver

www.lexiecarver.com

lexiecarver69@gmail.com

lexie@lexiecarver.com

ISBN 978-0-692-17957-4 (Paperback edition)

This is a work of fiction. Names, character, places and incidents either are the product of the author's imagination or are used fictitiously and any resemblance to actual persons, living or dead, business establishments, events or locales are purely coincidental.

Front cover image from Photoshock, ID:523572745, ra2studio

Cover design by "MerryBookRound" www.merrybookround.com

Book design by Lexie Carver

"Death Proof Inc.," and "Vampires Anonymous," were published in Sirens Call 'Scared Stiff' Vol 39

Printed and bound in the United States of America

First printing September 2018

Published by Lexie Carver

Visit www.lexiecarver.com

This is Dedicated to...

To my mother who inspired me to think big.

To my loving editor who was driven crazy over the course of these writings.

To my loyal dog, who was always there to offer love and licks when needed and sometimes some ambient barks.

To my friends who are all rockstars and badasses. Love you girls.

To all the horror movies that inspired me.

To Nix Toro who died too young. A close friend, a confidant, a powerhouse and a talented, darkly inclined woman with so many layers. You will be missed.

For all the women out there who love horror -- this one's for you.

Enjoy
XOXO

Contents

A Note to My Readers...

Thank you for purchasing this book. Inside you'll find a range of stories that are, as I like to call them, "horror-lite." There are stories that will make your heart race, make you think about the world around you, make you cry, or turn you on. Get in the mind of a killer, see love and speed dating from a unique perspective, hear a sales pitch with a way to live forever, go on a bus ride you'll never forget. See firsthand how powerful a mother's love is, read about vampire support groups, and many more stories. As with many of my stories, they aren't what they seem. They're clever tales with strong female characters fighting back against all odds. There's something for everyone in these stories with two erotica stories at the end. As they say, go out with a bang. There's even a whole new look for Hell itself -- the Devil as you've never seen him before. Welcome to Hell. Hope you enjoy your stay.

(Look for my future compilations and a novel coming soon.) Into the Dark, a collection of macabre poems by yours truly is out now in Kindle and print editions.

Now I know you're all curious about little old Lexie Carver. Well, I'm a feisty woman who lives out loud doesn't take any shit from anyone, a veritable badass. Living in the city is never easy, even on a tree-lined street. I'm a free-lance writer and I love writing fan fiction. My collection of macabre poems, *Into the Dark*, is now out in Kindle and print editions.

But enough about myself, what about you guys? I love to connect with fans and I love writing. Come say hi. Below are some my social media accounts.

Website: www.lexiecarver.com
Twitter: @Lexie_Carver
Email: LexieCarver69@gmail.com
lexie@lexiecarver.com
Facebook: lexiecarverthehorrorwriter
Tumblr: @roxy-davenport
Spotify: Lexie Carver

Previous Works

Into the Dark

Have a wonderful day. Tata my darlings.

XOXO

Lexie Carver

ONE

Death Proof Inc.

"Welcome everyone and thank you for attending. If you would be so kind as to put your phones on silent, we would greatly appreciate it. And please, no video recording. We can't show this to the general public, I'm sure you understand why. I've put together a PowerPoint presentation to further explain to new clients exactly what our firm does here. Please, stop me at any time if you have any questions."

The presenter stops speaking, and looks around the room at all the nervous faces in front of him, though I don't think anyone could be more nervous than I am.

My dad has Stage 4 cancer and without this, he'll be dead soon. He's everything I have in this world. I'm an only child and I refuse to live in a world without him. Death is everywhere in our society. Horror movies play on that exact fear. Some people embrace a fear of death and even death itself, while others are so crippled by it that they can't function. Me, I never thought about death until we heard the diagnosis. I lived in a world of privilege, protected from the ravages of the outside world. I didn't think death could get to me or my father. I just hope this company isn't full of crap. I've been to three other talks about how to live forever. One was even going on about blood. H*ow utterly disgusting and unhygienic. Really?*

I sip my coffee anxiously awaiting the continuation of the talk. Time goes slowly. I keep glancing over at my dad. My hands shake from the massive amounts of caffeine I've ingested, just to stay awake, to be able to take care of him.

The presenter starts speaking again, his voice melodious and calm. "Now, it is 2280 and we still don't have a cure for cancer. There have been a lot of recent advances in our society and many companies offer a chance to beat death but I offer you *forever.* And my claim unlike my competitors is the real deal. I don't offer you a measly couple of years like my competitors do. No. For the elite, such as yourselves, I offer you *forever.* The common people, well, they're cute in their struggle to survive, but why would we want to save people like them? Wouldn't we rather have a society of elites who live forever? The others would work for us and provide for the society we live in. The commoners don't have much to offer the world, except their dedication to their jobs, earning hardly anything. It's all rather endearing. You have to love those little worker bees. This project, this company, is all for you, the elite. Now, it is true that we don't have the full consent of the FDA. Since this is so outside 'normal, I don't think we ever will."

I speak up, raising my hand. "Um…are there any risks involved?"

"Very good question. I don't want to say no, but the risks are minimal. I see your father is quite sick and I assume the sickness is leaking into his soul. He is probably quite weak. The risk goes up if the patient is weak, but it's minimal. The reward greatly outweighs any concerns.

I have to hand it to this guy, he's a good salesman.

"The procedure is simple. Basically, we take your soul and place it in a younger body. We keep doing this *forever. You* decide when you've had enough *not* Mother Nature. *You* control your own destiny. You can be a god among men."

"Do you get to choose --," a meek voice spoke up.

"Your new body? Yes, of course, dear. There is a booklet in front of you with a list of healthy Americans. All the people listed in that booklet are downstairs. They are fed proper meals, of course, none of this vegan or vegetarian crap. They are given vitamins and daily exercise to make sure they're at their peak for our clients. You can pick any of them and can even come downstairs to look at them in person."

A business man asks, "What happens to the souls that are already in these people?"

"Honestly, why would you care? They're nothing. They rely on the government to help them out. They're not rich, they have no families. They're living a pitiful life, really. This would be a mercy killing."

"How do you do it? And how many times has it been done before?" I ask utterly intrigued about the possibilities. He was right, of course. Why would one care what happens to those unfortunates? We are the important ones. We are the ones with money. We control the fate of everyone.

"More good questions. You are the best clients so far. Of yes, I've done this before, many times. A person could run several times for the Presidency since they appear to be different people. But I've already said too much I'm afraid. The possibilities are endless. Now, the *how* is a bit complicated. I brought a video to show you."

The presenter snaps his finger and a very attractive woman smiles at us, the clients, before turning the lights off.

"That's my wife of 150 years. Doesn't look a day over 23, does she? Thank you, dear."

His wife bows to us in turn before pressing the button on the PowerPoint presentation.

"Now, as to how...well, there is an old black magic ritual that dates back to Salem, Massachusetts. A few of the people that were killed in the Salem Witch Trials were actually witches and they used this ritual to transfer their souls to another body before their flesh burned. The founder of Death Proof Inc. was one of those very witches and has graced us with the ingredients and the Latin ritual needed. It would always be done in front of her and her coven of witches to ensure that it is done correctly. She does every transfer personally."

My father inquired, "Are there any side effects?"

Even though I had asked the question already, my father needed to know specifically what would happen. He wanted to make sure this was his best chance for survival. I turn to look at him and hug him tightly. The presenter watches our interaction and his eyes visibly soften.

"Well, your soul is contained in a shell of sorts so, yes, sometimes there are side effects. Sometimes the person goes into a deep sleep for two weeks and wakes up refreshed and new. Some have migraines for a week. Some a slight stomach bug for a week, while others have no side effects at all. Of course, the sample size is rather small so it's hard to come up with percentages and risk analysis information. We're not quite sure why some people have side effects, and others don't. But we can assure you that the side effects are minimal."

"The price is 10 million, correct?" I ask confidently. This man may be lying, and the procedure may not work, but somehow, I feel confident and trust him. I have hope again and that is a precious thing indeed.

"Yes, in cash if you can. I do so hate having to fill out tax forms. As if the government doesn't have enough money. I mean we're all rich here and we deserve every penny, even if we didn't actually work for it. So let's screw the government and taxes and let's live forever. Who's with me?"

Everyone raises their hand including me. The presenter smiles, though I can't be sure if it's because of all the money we brought in our briefcases or because he would be saving all of us. Whatever the reason, I know this is our best chance.

"Follow me then and welcome to a brave new world."

―――――――――――――

TWO

Be Careful What You Wish For

Mara's shoes click-clacked on the cobblestones, echoing off the forlorn street, her heels acting as a strange loud harbinger signaling her whereabouts to every ne'er-do-well in the vicinity. Mara was taking a shortcut through an alleyway. The wind was enough to chill a person to the bone, not to mention the late hour. Taking the quicker path made sense, but there are always consequences to crossing an alleyway after midnight.

Mara tensed when she heard someone behind her. She slowly turned her head when she noticed a movement out of the corner of her eye. She saw a large shadow on the wall beside her, slowly looming over her. She froze when she heard several footsteps behind her. Whoever it was brought friends. *Great.*

Mara took a deep breath to steady herself before she started running as quickly as she could, bolting straight out of the alleyway. She could see cars in front of her. She was so close to getting away without a fuss when she was rudely shoved back into the alleyway by a strong force. She slammed into a very firm chest. Mara's feet were pulled clean off the ground. A strong arm wrapped around her middle. She screamed into the night, but the only people who heard it were already there with her. She subtly shook her head not to intervene. Then something scratchy fell over her eyes. There were no witnesses in a place like this, at a time like this. No one to help. No one was on the street, and hardly any cars were on the road. Familiar shadows moved in front of her, waiting and watching. She felt something scratchy dig into her wrists – rope, if she had to guess.

Mara was shoved unceremoniously into a van that had one of those disgusting soft rugs on the floor. *So very creepy.* She whirled around, as well as one can with a blindfold on and wrists restrained. Another man, closer to her this time, who had major hygiene issues, checked her bindings and tied her wrists tighter. She growled, which the men around her thought cute.

Her shock at the novel situation was quickly turning into anger at being made into a victim. She refused to play this role for much longer.

She smelled incense being lit and heard shuffling next to her. Then there was a crunching sound as if they were opening pages from an old tome. Mara heard them chanting all at the exact same time, in some weird language. Definitely, not the kind you learn in high school. Maybe what they thought was Latin? Who knows? Whatever it was sent chills down her spine. Bad enough they kidnap her and drag her off the street, but now rituals and chanting? That *definitely* wasn't good.

Mara tried to wiggle out of her confines, but the man directly behind her held her close to his chest in a vise-like grip. His sweaty, rough hands dug into the soft flesh of her shoulders. The bindings were tight, and her arms were starting to get sore. The man behind her was holding her so tightly she could feel the imprint of his body against hers. The more she struggled, the tighter he held her. She got the idea and disgust flashed across her face before a blinding rage settled upon it.

A man farthest from her spoke up and judging from the way his voice carried, he was probably close to the driver. His voice held frustration and incredulity in it. "Are you sure *she's* the one?"

"Yes, the boss says she is," the man beside her answered, more than a little peeved.

"Why *her*, though? She's just a slip of a girl. Too afraid to do much. Didn't even get a punch out," the man that held her to him stated in a teasing tone.

"You will all soon regret this," were the only words Mara desperately wanted to say but she held her tongue.

"Yeah, a lightweight," the man by the door replied in a scoff, the one whose foot kept bashing the door. That must be an uncomfortable place to sit. How right they were to be concerned that she might run or put up a fight.

"Hey, if the boss says she's the one, she's the one," the man near the driver reiterated. He then added, "Remember why we do this. This is all to serve our master."

That piqued Mara's interest. *These boorish men were doing all this to serve a master? And what master would that be?*

"Yes, to serve our master," they all stated in unison.

Mara frowned deeply under the blindfold. Speaking in unison? There was no reasoning with these men. They were all of one mind, all in the service of their "master." But what was their idea for young Mara?

The rest of the ride was spent in silence which honestly, Mara wasn't sure was better or worse than talking. At least when they talked, their eyes and thoughts were not focused on her. Even with the blindfold on, she could feel their gaze on her, their eyes roving up and down her figure. It made her sick to her stomach. Not to mention that comment about punching them. If they wanted a fight, she would be happy to offer it. She had tried to resist but it is quite difficult against a group of men.

The drive wasn't too long. Mara thought that maybe they went to a town close by. It was only an hour and a half drive which actually took three because they kept doubling back. How could she know that? She felt the vibrations of the car. She closed her eyes and felt how it moved, in what direction, the speed, etc. There are so many things one can notice when no one thinks you're watching.

The van made a cringe-worthy squeaking sound and then stopped, probably in a garage of some sort judging by the somewhat muffled footsteps sounding above her. Next came what can only be described as a boom, which Mara assumed were the doors opening, the back doors. A flickering light came into the van, but her blindfold was so oppressive that barely any light came through. She was still shrouded in darkness, which was likely the point. She could only make out vague, shadowy shapes in front of her.

"Be careful with the girl. We need her in mint condition or he'll have our heads," a new voice cautioned, likely the driver. His voice was rough with a slight accent she couldn't place, an accent he tried hard to disguise.

Mint condition? Huh, that's a new wrinkle.

She felt a rough, sweaty hand wrap around her upper arm, trying to pull her out of the van. Mara violently shook with disgust at being touched by the likes of him. With a growl, she drew her other foot back and kicked out as hard as she could.

There were shadows and shapes moving in front of her. She used the shadows as guides and shoved each shape into another until everyone seemed to be crying out in injury.

Mara ran out of the van, falling hard onto the concrete floor, since her hands were still tied to her back. She scraped her knees, her elbow was killing her, and her ankle felt off. *Perfect.* But none of that mattered, she had to get out of wherever this was. She had no idea whether she was running towards or away from this horrible scene but run she did.

She used the shadows to gauge distance and stopped whenever a dark shape seemed close. She stumbled through what she thought must be a house, a large house. She felt out the shapes in front of her. She had no idea who these people were or what their intentions were, but she wasn't buying the whole "mint condition" idea these creepy men were selling. *Concerned kidnappers? Give me a break!* Looking for a way out would be her best play and quickly, she had already broken two things on the way in.

She heard footsteps that sounded as if they were coming from every direction all at once. She stifled a scream. She refused to be this close to freedom, only to be found out because she couldn't keep quiet. *Damn my luck.* And if she did get discovered, well, she wasn't going to make it easy for them. She was going to fight.

Mara walked all through the house until she got to what felt like a door. The second she touched it, she was propelled into a room hidden by a bookcase. It was as though her proximity to it sucked her in. And sadly, she had been so close to the front door. *Stupid magical doors!*

"Hello, so nice of you to join us," a new voice stated, a voice she hadn't heard before. None of the voices from the car ride over here sounded like this man. This had to be the fearless leader. His voice commanded respect and dripped with malice, in a deep register.

"The leader I presume," Mara noted in an exasperated tone.

"Clever girl," the leader teased. He looked at Mara with a smirk. "Yes, that's me. Now I assume you're wondering why you're here. We'll get to that in a second. Oh, how rude of me. Rufus, would you be so kind as to take off that scratchy fabric? Wouldn't want our guest of honor to be more uncomfortable than necessary."

"No, we wouldn't want that," Mara replied sarcastically.

The laugh the leader let out was chilling, but Mara was unimpressed and unaffected. Honestly, she'd heard scarier. She simply glared at him through her blindfold.

The second the blindfold was off her eyes, she frowned. These were the morons who kidnapped her? They looked like rejects from a bad horror movie. One was a balding, heavily tattooed, brick shithouse of a 50-year-old, who probably still lived with his mother, two wannabe rockers, one man cosplaying in Victorian garb, and a hipster. What the hell was going on? This was kind of insulting! Help *is* really hard to find, apparently. The leader himself, looked like a suave, debonair monster, a vampire you would willingly throw yourself to. What an eclectic bunch.

"Good help is hard to find?" Mara quipped, not being able to stop herself.

The leader smirked at her rather bold comment.

"Any chance you could undo my wrists as well?" she asked with a shrug. *Never hurts to try.*

The leader fake-pouted, feigning sympathy. "No, dearie. Can't have you getting hurt now," the leader uttered in a sweet, melodic tone.

"Oh, do get on with it already. What was with the door that sucked me in. Huh?" Mara replied in a frustrated growl.

"Oh yes, forgive me, we're Satanists by the way and well, we can't have you leave. The door was part of a protection ritual. Wouldn't want you going out there and getting yourself hurt."

"Oh, how thoughtful, looking out for little old me. You wouldn't mind untying me then since my wrists are hurting, would you?"

"Cute. As for what we're doing… well, we're trying to call up the great lord. We called upon him in a dark ancient ritual of blood to name his vessel and lo and behold, he chose you."

"I think I would be better…" a Satanist in the back, piped up.

Mara rolled her eyes at that. As if anyone would want that man for well… much of anything. *A vessel, him? Please.*

"Don't you dare presume to know better than our dark lord. In his infinite wisdom, he chose *her* to be his mouthpiece, his *vessel.* We have to respect that. She will be the mother of all evil."

Everyone bowed to Mara as they chanted, "Mother of all evil."

Oh, you've got to be kidding me! They called up someone and it led them to me? Well, isn't that interesting."

That was when Mara couldn't take it anymore and started to laugh. It started out as a small giggle and crescendoed into a loud ruckus of sounds that were so inhuman and animalistic that it shook everyone in the room to their core. It broke pictures and glasses. Her red eyes bore through the darkness around her. A single snap broke the twine around her wrists. All the injuries she sustained, like a sprained ankle, were now healed. There was a power coursing through her, under her skin, lighting it up in an orange, healing glow.

"Forgive me for laughing. You all look so serious and I wouldn't want to insult anyone's beliefs but really? The devil would want you to kidnap random women? *Frighten* them? *Terrorize* them … only to *what?* Then finally *kill* them? He is trapped forever in Hell just feeding off of scraps that Satanists give him? *Really?* He's just biding his time until a *human* helps him out?"

She walked over to the small altar they made, flashing her red glowing eyes at them. She watched in satisfaction as they slowly stepped away from her. She held up the spell and read it quickly by the candlelight. It was a pathetic spell. There was no way this would have called up anything. It was some garbage found on a search engine. Not *real* witchcraft. Yet Mara had felt a magical disturbance and appeared by the alleyway to investigate. This fake spell could cause a magical disturbance? Curious little scrap of paper.

The light flickering on her face revealed two faces superimposed onto each other: a gorgeous but frail human woman and a darker more demonic face, a face that was as white as a sheet with sunken black eyes and endless tiny teeth littering a giant bloody mouth. Her eyes snapped to the acolyte regarding her.

"And what? This crappy ritual you got off the internet is going to call up the devil himself and he goes into some poor human you butchered? Pathetic, *really*! And then he grants you powers? Greedy, power hungry morons."

"Lady, I have no idea how you--."

"You moronic simpletons. How do you know that the Devil is a man? Women have always been better temptresses than any man. And if God is a man wouldn't it be fitting for the Devil to be a woman? You think the Devil is but one thing, male or female, human or demon?"

Everyone froze in the room. The shadows cast an eerie projection on the wall. It was as if all the shadows gathered together, and formed in the shape of a man, who was slowly standing up. Suddenly, a gust of wind blew out all the candles. A gust of wind in a stone walled, basement with no windows.

"You know I really committed to the victim role. Your shock and awe proves it. I acted scared, I screamed even. I deserve an Emmy. I didn't use my powers once, scouts honor. I actually left the blindfold and bindings on and felt up the wall. What a night! I just didn't want to spoil the surprise until I figured out what you *idiots* were up to. And wow, am I *not* impressed! How did that spell, and *you* create a magical disturbance, anyway?"

Mara moved like a cat, toying with a mouse, slow and predatory. "Now don't get me wrong, boys, I love a little sacrifice, a little blood… but *come on*. I don't ask you to kill innocent women for me.

You idiots don't have the power to call me up even if I were taking a vacation in Hell. You're *humans*. You're no match for a centuries-old being. *Please*. The utter hubris of your species is *disgusting, pathetic even*.

I've been on Earth for a long-time, morons. I've whispered lies in the ears of generals to incite wars, whipped crowds to murder and tempted men to create chaos. I watched with glee as you tore yourselves apart, as you killed in my name, slaughtered innocents, wrote books about me, thought about me, feared me, lived for me. It's all rather touching, I'm in the collective unconscious!

But enough is enough. I can't very well be responsible for every evil act in this stupid dust cloud of a world. At some point, you have to acknowledge that it's the evil in mankind and not me doing it. Even *I* can't be *everywhere* all at once.

And I definitely don't need morons as my sycophantic followers. I deserve a better class of followers, a better class of criminals to call my own. Now for punishment…Well, my shape-shifting hellhound is hungry and so is my bodyguard. Hmm… boys, we have six morons here. Divide them up equally and bring me their souls when you're done."

Her hellhound and bodyguard bowed to Mara and she smiled at both of them in turn. Mara left with a smile on her face, as she slowly walked up the basement stairs. The cries and screams from her would-be kidnappers, died out the further she went into the apartment. She closed her eyes relishing their fear and suffering before she went off to explore what hidden gems might be in this apartment. No sense in not looking around. Maybe there was something of import here.

When her henchmen were done, they went to look for her. They presented her with shiny balls of light which she consumed in a heartbeat, her eyes glowing amber. Nothing like a soul pick-me-up for a slow week. Her hellhound, now in human form, blood dripping down his chiseled chest, kneeled before his Queen. Mara looked at him and pet his head. "Such a good puppy. I'm going to reward you tonight. I have a fun idea I'd love to try with you. You haven't forgotten your safe word, have you?"

"Chocolate hammock," he said in delight.

Mara chuckled darkly, "Such a *deliciously odd* phrase for something as dark as we are. I utterly love it, darling. I say the same thing every time, *I know*. Good boy."

Her second henchman stood in the doorway, nodding to his mistress.

"Very well. Come along now. We have so much to do. There's nothing at all interesting here. Just know-nothing punks trying to become someone by calling up little old me. If I had a nickel for every time- -!" she growled out, before snapping her fingers and teleporting them all to her lavish penthouse suite in her favorite hotel.

Finally, back to luxury, the kind that always washed away the idiosyncrasies of being an everlasting fallen angel/demon. She smiled, content to be home. Well, her second home, Hell was well ... *Hell*. She liked her penthouse suite much better than dealing with Hell's paperwork and needy demons vying for her attention.

She smiled at her minions, including her lovely secretary, who just walked in. Mara settled in for a night of debauchery, sure that after tonight, she'd be right as rain.

After all, tomorrow was a busy day and she couldn't stay mad at those peons who attempted to summon her. She was the Queen of Hell and had larger concerns than moronic humans.

Be careful what you wish for, dear reader. I'm always listening.

———————————————

THREE

Vampires Anonymous

"Hello, everyone. My name is Lainie. Welcome to Vampires Anonymous, where we're trying to learn how to control our urges and live among humans. As we do every week, let's go around the room, and say a little something about ourselves. And welcome to the new members. Would you like to start, Paul?"

"Sure. Hi, I'm Paul and I've been human sober for about three years."

Everyone clapped at his achievement. Paul smiled at each person in turn before proceeding.

"It's been a long road, and I'd be happy to be someone's sponsor. I know how hard it is. It took a long time to get to a comfortable place. Things are going well with me and Angie. She doesn't suspect a thing. I eat when she's asleep. She's actually the reason *why* I stay sober. The thought that if I don't eat regularly, and I slip up, I could lose her or worse *kill* her? Well, that's all the incentive I need to keep on the human-free diet, as I like to call it."

There were a few chuckles from the group before Ethan stood up to address everyone.

"Hi, my name is Ethan. I'm a new member, just joined today, actually. Can I ask you a question, Paul?"

"Any member can ask any other member whatever you want. This is a safe place for all. We're here to support each other," Lainie offered with a kind smile.

"Thank you...Uh...well...Isn't the diet hard? I don't know how you do it. I slipped up yesterday. I didn't kill anyone, I swear. But my fangs came out. I went...I went into a club. I made out with this girl and then boom; my fangs were out. I'm not proud of it and uh... well...I drank a little from her. She was okay after I left, just a little weak. I just...I slipped. I don't want to feed on humans. I really don't. The hunger, it just got too strong. It took me over. I was able to bring myself back, but I'm terrified that the next time I won't be able to."

"That's okay, Ethan, everyone here understands what you're going through. We've all been there. The hunger is always going to be there. You have to choose to ignore it, and focus on what you want, which is to live among humans. I'm glad she was okay, and the fact that you had the strength to pull yourself back is an extraordinary thing. Not many would be able to. That's the first step. This is why we have these meetings, and this support system, but when that happens, what are you supposed to do?"

"I'm supposed to call you or my sponsor," Ethan said in a shaky voice, head down.

"Yes, exactly. No need to be ashamed. This is just to remind you of the protocol so that next time, we can help prevent any biting on your end. You already know the procedure — that's half the battle. You have to pick one of us, any one of us to call. We will talk you down and remind you of why you're fighting. We would have instructed you to leave the second your fangs came out and go into an alleyway to talk to us. Let me just remind everyone here that any slip up is bad for our kind. If the police suspect vampires, we're all going to be in trouble and they might even disband this group. This is a resource for vampires, let's not let that happen."

"Of course. I'm sorry," Ethan stated with a tremor in his voice, his emotions betraying him for a moment.

The group responded with the slogan, "Don't be sorry, be smart."

Ethan smirked and nodded at Lainie. "Yes, ma'am."

Lainie smiled warmly at Ethan. "Good. Thank you for sharing, Ethan, and welcome to the group. I'm happy you're here. Amanda, I believe it's your turn now."

"Oh yes, hi. I'm Amanda, obviously. Um...yeah, so I've been human sober for a long time. I'm married with kids. They don't know what I am. I drink in front of them and say it's tomato juice. Humans don't happen to like that very much. And even the healthy ones don't want to drink straight tomato juice. I find for me, it's easier to drink among humans. They eat and drink at least three times a day, and so do I. It makes it normal for me. No hiding, no drinking in the shadows. Monsters don't come out in the open and that's where I drink. I have a normal life, and the urges are kept at bay with the routine, and the normalcy of everything. I drink it with the insufferable PTA moms, at sports games and on date nights. It's really a great method. I buy blood from a supplier. He gives me mostly animal blood with some human plasma from hospitals, for those really bad days when only human blood will do. I put it all in giant pitchers and juice boxes labeled 'Tomato Juice.' My family just thinks I'm health conscious."

"How are you able to—"

"Function, Ethan? I'd been lonely for a while before I found my husband. I've been going to this program regularly. Things will get easier after a while. I'm 200 years old, Ethan. You're a young one. Don't beat yourself up over it, it gets easier. Trust me. I love this human, and marriage is a human convention that they prefer to adopt when they find love. I never imagined kids, and without the amazing vampiric doctors, and the specific breakthroughs in vampiric fertility, it would never have been a reality. You know what humans think of vampires. It's easier to just pretend. I can't lose the kids or my husband. I couldn't bear it, so I do what I have to, to keep them. It's as simple as that."

"But the cravings..." Ethan inquired.

"I drink mostly pig's blood instead of human. The only human blood I drink is from blood drives. I can give you the number of my supplier. He offers discounts to newbies. He's a great guy. Anyway, pig's blood is not as sweet, but it does the trick. It provides all the nourishment a growing vampire needs. Drink as much as you need. There are some days when I need seven drinks, and some days when three is fine. Feed your urges safely, that's the key. Now for the taste, well, you can always mask it with ginger, a little brown sugar and vanilla extract. I know it's a weird combination, but it works, and it tastes delicious."

Lainie's eyes lit up at the mention of a tasty recipe. "Oh, that's a good one, Amanda, I personally use cherry syrup, and graham cracker crust, and bake it into a pie. I have a giant sweet tooth."

Amanda chuckled at that. "Remind me to come over for pie sometime, Lainie."

"Anytime, Amanda. Actually, I'm having a party next week and would love for all of you to come. There *will* be pie."

"But the urges …" Ethan implored, desperate to know the secret that everyone else seemed to have.

"Ethan, everyone here is ready and willing to help. Use us as a resource, that's what this group is meant for. This was made to help our kind transition into a world built for humans, to exist peacefully side-by-side. We don't have to be the monsters they think we are and we don't have to hide in the shadows.

The urges will go away, but you need a reason; love, morality, something bigger than the urges, to give yourself over to. A reason to remind yourself in those difficult moments why you're fighting so hard. Only *you* can provide that reason. If you slip up, they will find you and kill us all. Self-preservation could be a reason. Think about what drives you and call one of us tomorrow. Use us as resources. Now, here's another newbie. Lisa, right?"

"Yes, hi. My name is Lisa. My vampire doctor suggested I come here."

"Dr. McClintock?" Paul asked.

"Yes," Lisa replied with a small nod.

"Oh, he's the best," Amanda offered.

"Yes. Well, I'm here because, well, I just recently got turned. My sire dropped me off at the doctors and I don't want to be evil."

"Oh, dear me. I hate sires like that. I'm sure the Vampire

Council will recall him. That is not allowed. You've indeed come to the right place, dear. We are the go-to for all vampire services in the community. Here is a list of all the services that our kind may need," Lainie stated as she handed Lisa a colorful brochure.

"Have you eaten?" Lainie asked.

"Only a little at the doctors."

"You poor thing. Okay, the Raven Cottage is where you must go next, Lisa. They tend to newbies and set you up with a caseworker and a chaperone, who is to accompany you on all outings for the first 50 years. Ethan, if you'd like the same, go to the Raven Cottage. I will call a vampire car service to take you both there. There will be blood provided for you both in the car if you'd like."

Both Lisa and Ethan nodded. Lainie took a moment to text the car service. She didn't want to make the newbies uncomfortable and thought texting over calling would be best.

Text: We have two newbies. Desperate here. Need a strong driver and blood provided in the back. Hurry."

Lainie returned to the group with a smile. "Let's cut this meeting short to attend to our two new members. This was a very good session. Welcome to the vampire community and to this group, Lisa and Ethan. Stay safe and stay smart everyone."

"Stay safe and stay smart," everyone replied.

The limo arrived immediately. Lainie shepherded the two newly turned vampires into the limo, before any passersby could see that the bloodlust had made their eyes turn violet. Not a human color to say the least.

"Blood is in the refrigerator, both pig and human. Human snacks like crackers and cookies are in the cabinet to your left, Lisa."

Lainie closed the door and walked quickly over to the driver. "Take them directly to the Raven Cottage. Don't stop for anything. Whatever they say, don't listen. Make sure they get to the cottage."

The driver looked a little apprehensive. He hadn't driven newbies for a hundred years. But he nodded all the same, a steely determination coming over his face. "Of course, ma'am."

"Thank you."

Amanda, Paul and Lainie watched the car leave, wobbling a bit as it drove over the cobblestones and sped off onto the dark highway. "I always feel so good being able to help our kind like that, but our group keeps getting smaller and smaller and—."

Amanda wrapped her arm around Lainie offering her some much-needed comfort. "They were referred here by McClintock. He's doing his job, Lainie. More will come. We can only help those who want to be helped. We can't help those who refuse to stop drinking humans dry."

"Yes, more will come. McClintock is doing his job and I believe we have a large ad out in the *Vampire Weekly*, the only vampire-centric newspaper. I get upset when I read vampire deaths as well, Lainie, but we're helping the community. As Amanda said, we're helping those we can, and the ones we can't help get recalled by the all-wise Council. We do our part. We can't save everyone all the time. That just isn't possible.

"Yes, the whole business in the town square yesterday evening...well, no talking, no *group* could have prevented that *massacre*. *Animals*, the lot of them. I'm happy they were recalled. If any vampire ever deserved a recall, it was those monsters. We couldn't have saved those vampires because they were beyond saving. The system somehow failed them before we could ever have helped them. You don't become that way by yourself, you're made that way after centuries of loneliness, with no help or resources. Sometimes people fall through the cracks," Amanda offered.

Lainie and Paul nodded as they all stood there in silence for a bit before Amanda spoke up.

"I really am sorry to leave you two especially on that note, but I don't want my husband wondering where his wife went off to. He'll be home soon."

"Oh course, Amanda. Same time next week? You too, Paul?"

"Same time," both Paul and Amanda said in unison.

They all walked away into the night, a common secret shared among them as they left to pretend to be human once more, secretly longing for next week to come around again when they could be their true selves.

———————————————

FOUR

Exact Change

Glass shattered all around Cody. She shrieked as small slivers of glass cut her soft skin while other lay on her clothes. She took deep breaths in and out, trying to calm herself. Her hands were shaking.

With no glass in the windows, the car was exposed to the outside and the brutal cold of the night, making Cody shiver mercilessly against it. She tried to concentrate on driving. She could make it, she *had* to make it. So what if all the glass in both front windows and the small side mirror were smashed? She was on a dark desolate highway, so it didn't matter if she didn't have much peripheral vision. There were no other cars here. She just had to make it further and Cody had a full tank of gas. She could make it.

Ignoring her fear, Cody pushed the pedal down all the way, soaring down the dark highway, swerving in and out of lanes, trying to evade the thing following her, whatever it was, as it threw something toward her car. Cody kept her mind focused on driving and her eyes on the road in front of her. Whatever it was throwing made pinging and crunching sounds when it hit her car. That couldn't be good.

Cody felt an ominous sense of dread and was compelled to look behind her to try to find out who was chasing her. I mean what could be following her and how was it blending in to the night? She didn't see anything, no other cars, no shapes in the night, nothing. Cody turned back around but something was dragging her attention to the backseat. She glanced quickly in the rearview mirror but saw nothing save for a few small shadows. But something had to be here with her. Cars don't make loud sounds on their own and glass doesn't break itself. Was it invisible? Cody was on the highway so that meant whatever it was, it was driving an invisible car? Or maybe it could walk at 60 miles per hour? Yeah, both explanations sounded equally ridiculous. But yet she knew someone, or something was there with her.

The cold seemed more insistent, the longer she drove. It was like she was in a meat locker or something. She was shivering behind the wheel, nervously looking around in the dark for her boogeyman. The darkness around her seemed like an entity in itself. It seemed to engulf all light around her in a solid mass of darkness. Cody's headlights did nothing to light the way ahead of her.

Was it safe to pull over? Had she lost whatever it was? She'd been driving at 60 mph for the past ten minutes. There was no chance that it was still following her, right?

Cody slowly took her eyes off the road for one second, only a second, to look behind her and the car jumped, making a rattling sound. Then a burning smell followed. A smell that was so pervasive that even in the semi-open space it felt like she was choking to death. Cody's lungs felt like they were on fire.

She saw shadows approaching the car, her car. More broken glass, this time from the back window. Then there was a distinct whooshing sound that seemed to fill the car. Her breath came out in gasps.

The shadows in her backseat started to take form slowly, coming together before Cody's eyes. She started in shock and horror, her eyes on the mirror as she saw the shadows slowly take a human form with piercing eyes.

Cody kept driving although constantly hitting the side of the road. It's rather hard to focus on driving when you're terrified and there's a strange entity in your backseat. Cody tried to keep her eyes on the road, but they kept darting behind her to glance at the shadow. What was it and what was it doing? It seemed like it was just sitting there.

Little by little skin and bones started to appear until a grotesque figure of a burned human face stared back at her. She gulped, panicking because of the creature in her backseat. It took everything she had to continue driving and not give in to fear.

The thing had a voice, a mangled and strained deep voice but a voice nonetheless. "Cody, stop the car and come with me. You --."

Come with it? It must be joking. And what's with its voice?

A piercing scream filled the car, stopping the apparition from speaking with her any further. It took a moment for Cody to realize *she* was the one screaming. She could barely breathe; her heart was beating so fast, she swore she could hear it. She took a shuddering breath as she tried desperately to come up with a solution.

I can't outrun a shadow, can I? Do shadows run? He's sort of a person but…. this car is breaking down. Whatever he threw at it, damaged it. I won't be able to outrun him. And he can always reach over and grab me in the car. I need to get away. NOW. OK, think. I'm in the middle of nowhere. Maybe getting out now is my best option? Wait a minute, how the hell did he know my name? He said Cody! What the hell is it? Is it even a he? Wait, focus girl. You're an intelligent grad student and you can't think in a crisis? Oh great. Social work is a great major then. Wait -- a shadow. He's a shadow. Weakness. Think about it. Oh shit, he's getting closer. He's moving forward. Anything. Throw anything girl! Damn it!

Cody looked around in her car for something solid, anything, finding only her college textbook. That would have to do.

Cody threw it at his head and he groaned at the impact of the book. *Good, he's dazed.* Cody slammed on the breaks and stopped the car. He let out a terrifying growl when the forward force threw him against the back of the front seat. *Should have worn his seatbelt. Ha. When attacking victims in a car, always be prepared Mr. Shadow. OK, he's distracted. He's a shadow. What do shadows fear?* Cody ducked down grabbing the flashlight. *You can't have a shadow if there's light, can you?* The apparition loomed behind her a hair's breath away. His putrid, strangely warm, breath ghosted over her skin.

Cody closed her eyes and readied herself. If she was going to die, she was going to face it head on. In one quick movement she opened her eyes and turned on the flashlight full blast. She turned around and jumped into the backseat following the apparition as it screamed for mercy, throwing its hands up in submission.

Cody stood over him, menacing *him* now. The apparition kept screaming and seemed to get smaller and smaller. He wasn't so scary now.

Just at that moment, a rock came sailing through the window, narrowly missing her head. Either the person had crappy aim or it was meant as a warning and not as an execution. She was in the middle of nowhere at 2 am on a desolate highway and now, what? There were two enemies here trying to kill her? Two enemies in the space of five minutes? That's got to be a record. She really had no luck. Or she pissed off the wrong person? Cody couldn't remember having any enemies much less enemies that would go to these lengths.

The apparition in front of her had clearly been wounded by the light. One second to quickly glance over at the road wouldn't make a difference, right?

Cody moved the flashlight up to look out of her broken back window only to see nothing. She rolled her eyes and sighed dramatically. *Gotta love killers that play hide and seek.* There was no dirt upturned, no footsteps, no leaves or grass rustling and no tire treads. There was no sign that anyone left the car or even came close to it. There was no sign of anyone else out there except the shadow in the backseat and Cody. *How can you wipe away your footfalls in seconds? People can't vanish in seconds. And rocks don't throw themselves. How do you kill something you can't see? I got wounding them down pat but killing them is another matter.*

Cody threw the flashlight back at the apparition in her backseat. At least she could wound this one. He made a growling sound and shrunk more before Cody thought fleeing might be the best option. She nearly tore off the back door to get out. She tripped over something. *Great.* She had to get out of the car and away. The vehicle was making her a target somehow. That was it, right? *I'm a good person, a great student. Helpful even. I donate to charity, give to homeless people. I worked at a shelter for a whole year. I don't have any enemies. Especially not shadow people. What the hell?! I took track in school so running it is. Try and catch me now.*

Cody left everything, her entire life was in that car, *literally,* but all she cared about now was getting away from that thing. *When* she was safe, not *if,* she would come back for her things.

Her feet hit the pavement at a steady pace. Cody was never happier that she always wore sneakers.

That horrifying disfigured creature cocked his head, sighed deeply and then let out a horrifying shriek that sounded like a bear in a blender. Cody just kept running, putting all of her fear into it, this one act, running as fast as she could. She looked back just as she rounded a corner and saw more of them.

That must have been a backup call. Shit! Just what I need. Remind me why I thought driving all night, alone no less, was a good idea?

The more she ran, the darker the road got. How was that even possible? Maybe it was the monster's doing. But Cody literally couldn't see in front of her; she was running blind just hoping that she was still the only person on the road. There had to be a house, a store, something up ahead. If she could just run fast enough, she'd be safe.

The apparitions started to lose solid form and turned into shadows slinking along the slick road towards her. They made high-pitched wailing sounds as they got closer to her. Cody screamed until she had no breath in her, not that anyone would be able to hear or help her. But no harm in screaming anyway, right? There was no lighted place in sight, no help was coming.

Sunrise. Yeah. The sun would stop them. I'd be safe but...uh...yeah, it's like 15 minutes past 2 am. I'd say I'm some ways away from sunrise, so yeah, not going to outrun them in time for that. I can't run for four hours straight. But I'm not going to a be a victim either. Options.... Wait a minute what is that? Is that a sign? I can barely see it through the fog and darkness. It looks like a white metal something...Wait a minute it is a sign. In the middle of nowhere? Huh?

Cody ran even faster, running to that sign. It had to lead somewhere, mean something. People would be coming, she'd be safe, she had to make it. The shadows were gaining on her every second. She squinted her eyes, so she could read the sign. It was a bus stop. A bus stop in the middle of nowhere? Where did it go? Not that it mattered, anywhere away from those creatures would be ideal.

It was dangerous taking a bus to who knows where, but it was better than the alternative. There was a place to wait and there was light! It was in a glass enclosure with a seat and a LIGHT. A LIGHT. The shadow was close enough to touch her. He sensed she was close to getting out of his reach and grabbed at her. She dove to the safety of the lighted bus stop. She landed unceremoniously on the floor under the lamp. She slowly got up and sat directly under the light. The shadow made that horrifying sound again.

The other shadows swirled around her trying to break the glass or the light or both. Small pounding sounds filled her ears. Cody closed her eyes trying to focus on something else. Cody needed a rest, she couldn't run just yet. The shadows were all around her trying to get her. The light was flickering but there wasn't anything to do but wait. Wait and hope that help arrived. She had done what she could. Now she had to hope the bus would arrive in time.

The light above her head swayed dangerously. The pounding got more and more insistent. The glass started to break in some places as if there were something heavy weighing down on it.

The light above her flicked again, the bulb dangerous close to burning out. Out of the mist to her left she heard tires screeching and something blue came into her view. It had to be a bus. She was saved. She stood up on the bench jumping up and down hoping to get the driver's attention.

The pounding got worse. She screamed as some glass rained down on her, tearing her clothes and re-opening several deep cuts on her arm.

The next second the bus came to a screeching halt and stopped directly in front of her. The light from the bus drove the shadows back so she could step in. The second Cody got in, the door sealed shut with a muted thump sound.

Cody glanced behind her and saw that the creatures had broken the lamp, plunging the bus stop into darkness. The shadows were merging together to form humanoid creatures yet again.

A shadowy creature reached the door of the bus. Its solid but strangely shadowy hand leaving a sticky dried blood residue on the window. Its eyes bore into Cody's soul or, so it seemed to her. She shivered at its intense gaze.

The doors were closed locking Cody into her decision. Boy, did she hope it was the right one.

The bus driver looked at her woefully, taking in her torn clothes, the gashes and cuts on her arms and neck and the look on her face. He showed but a moment of sympathy for her. He switched back so fast into an indifferent look that she wasn't sure if she had really seen any sympathy in the first place. Now he looked bothered, like she was holding him up and picking her up was such a distasteful thing to do. Cody, unsure of what was happening, offered him a meek smile, hoping to offset his sour mood.

"Exact change," he said in a monotone voice. He pointed to the machine where he was expecting her to put the money in. "This isn't a free service lady. I ain't nobody's knight in shining armor. You pay, you stay."

Cody suppressed an eye-roll. The shadows were right there demanding entrance. The glass on the doors didn't budge, it was reinforced somehow. *Comforting to know. Of course, with psychotic beings intent on killing me, the bus driver has to hassle me for exact change. Is he kidding?! Takes all kinds I suppose. I hope I have exact change.*

Cody let out a panicked whine as she dropped to her knees in front of him, almost kneeling before him. She threw everything out of her pockets and found change. She always forgot to put change in her piggy bank and was never happier about it than at this moment.

"Come on lady, we don't got all day," the driver barked at her.

Cody placed the change on the floor, ignoring his demands to hurry up. The moment she had enough, she stood up and flew over to the machine to put all the coins in. The driver nodded apathetically and started moving away. She breathed a huge sigh of relief. *Whew!* She was damn lucky she had exact change.

The bus was moving so fast that Cody fell backwards onto the rubber mat on the floor of the bus. The driver could care less and soon enough was speeding down the road. *He desperately needs some lessons in manners, thank you very much.* Cody glared at the back of his head.

The shadow creatures screamed and flung themselves onto the bus hoping to break some part of it. Lights came out from the sides and back of the bus, chasing any residual shadows away. *Ok, so maybe whatever this bus is, wherever it's going, this was the right decision? Let's hope so. Have to look for a seat now.*

Cody took a shaky breath and slowly stood up grabbing the metal pole tightly with both hands. She slowly scanned the people on the bus. Cody suddenly wasn't sure this was such a great idea after all. There seemed to be an invisible line of freaky twisted people and then normal people. Was that common on a bus at 2:25? Who knows? Cody was usually asleep or driving at that time. She very rarely took public transportation of any kind and definitely not at night. But in this case, there was clearly no other option. This was actually her first time on a bus.

On the freaky side of the bus, which was the back of the bus, there was a woman with blood all over her face who was muttering to herself in the corner, a young woman covered with dirt who was completely out of it, and an old man in the back who was talking with a woman no more than 18, who looked petrified of him, an ex of hers maybe. In the corner, there was a man who looked like he stepped right out of the Victorian era. Next to him was a man with pieces of skin hanging off and a man with a burned face sat to his right. A woman sat next to him with blood on her hands literally. She kept rocking back and forth singing a nursery rhyme. That area of the bus was enough to creep out even the most hardened horror lover.

On the other side, next to the driver, it was a completely different story: a couple sat muttering to each other, talking and kissing as if nothing was wrong. A woman next to them was reading a book but the way the woman was holding it, Cody couldn't make out the title. The woman seemed to be smiling as she read it, so it was likely a personal favorite of hers. The man across from where Cody was standing was listening to music and smiling. The man behind him was drawing everyone and the couple behind him were playing a game of Poker. Cody quickly decided to sit on the normal side of the bus, next to the kissing couple. The second she sat down everyone on the bus including the driver stared at her as if this was the most important thing in the world. She gulped and gave the couple a sheepish smile and to her surprise, the woman took her hand and smiled warmly back at her.

"We've all been there. First time, right? Never been on the bus before?"

Ever or just this one? "Is it that obvious?"

She smiled sweetly at her before letting go of Cody's hand. "It's OK dear. We're on the good side. We mean you no harm. Welcome to the bus, honey. I'm Fraulein Mariya and this is Robert."

"Cody, just me, single," she confessed.

"I'm sorry to hear that. Maybe when the bus stops, you'll find someone. This is just the beginning."

"The beginning of what?" Cody questioned, utterly confused.

"Oh, dear me. No spoilers, honey," Fraulein Mariya replied.

Cody was beyond frustrated. Finally, she found a person who knew what was going on and she couldn't tell her? *Come on. Fine, I'll change the subject. Maybe if I cozy up to her, she might be a tad more talkative.* "Robert isn't a German or Russian name." *Wow, good job. Talk about her man. Real non-sequitur. Yeah, great. That came out really gruff. That's what happens when I'm denied the truth lady!*

"No, it isn't, he's American, I'm not, but we make it work. We love each other very much and I'm so happy we're able to do this together. We've been on here for a while."

That's touching, really lady. Where's the truth? Almost got killed here. Hello! "Stop being cryptic and tell me where this bus is going?" *So much for building a rapport. There I go being a bulldog. Damn it! Oh well.*

"You really don't know?" The woman inquired, incredulously.

If I knew, why would I be asking you? Cody shook her head. "No. I have no idea. Just got on to avoid those shadow peeps."

"This is the end honey, the end of the line," Mariya said gently as she placed a hand over Cody's.

"So, the bus doubles back? The end of the line like we're headed towards the bus warehouse?"

"No. The existential end of the line. You're dead. We're all dead," Mariya declared.

"What?! No, I'm not dead. Are you crazy? Are you drunk or something? What kind of joke is that? It's not funny by the way. I'm alive I evaded--."

"The shadows and it's good you did. They're not shadows, dear. They're ruined, tortured, damned souls. They're mindless creatures that just want to bring others the same pain as they are in. If they had caught you, you'd have been tormented and sent to torment others. A kind of living Hell. The driver heard your call and came as quickly he could."

"What?" Cody growled, rage bubbling up. *I can't possibly be dead, can I?*

"This is the hard part, honey. Think. *Really think* about what happened to you."

Cody looked around the bus again focusing on everyone's clothes. Everyone was wearing old fashioned clothes except for her. It was like a fashion museum right here in the bus. Everyone couldn't be cosplaying as an elaborate joke just for her. No way anyone could rig that up. But was she really dead? The blood on their hands, the confusion, the psychosis, the clothes, it all pointed to the logical conclusion that these people were dead, and they've been on the bus a long time. What had she gotten herself into?

"Some of them have been dead for hundreds of years. It's hard to get off the bus. To face what happened and so the bus just keeps moving endlessly. I think we're ready to get off now, finally. Thank you, Cody. I think it is about time I face death."

Just at that moment, the bus screeched to a halt. Cody was barely able to stay in her seat. *What the hell is up with this driver?*

The bus driver spoke loudly and clearly into the intercom. "Hell, we're in hell. Will the following people please leave the bus: Steven, Anna, Thomas, Abby, Lisa, David, and Adrian. I will wait here for exactly five minutes. Please look around and make sure to take all of your belongings with you."

"This is really Hell?" Cody asked, looking around at the ominous landscape before them.

"Well, the gateway to Hell. You get off the bus and then walk up to those black gates. It's the doorway, but good souls like us can't physically get out of the bus here. It's like a wall is in front of us. We can get to the door of the bus, but we wouldn't be able to walk out. Damned souls just go right through. I only know all this because I tried. I mean how can you not be curious about what it's like, right? All we know is there's a smoking hot woman outside, checking names. That's about it. It's kind of sad, you know. The bus driver drives over here and no ever gets off. I don't blame them. It's easy to do evil but not easy to pay the price. It means you have to remember, truly remember, what you did and accept it to get off the bus. That's a hard pill to swallow."

Cody saw the shadows at the gates. They saw her in the bus and tried to force the gate open to get to her.

"Cooodddy. Cooooddddy," they called after her.

The perky blonde demon with the clipboard shouted at them in some unknown language. Her focus shifted as she shouted at Cody from her desk, her voice loud, clear and actually kind of melodic.

"I apologize, dear, those shadows just don't know when to quit. You don't belong here but if you want to get off the bus I can make it worth your while. Take care of your family, give you power, make you a clipboard demon just like me. No torture that way. You express a desire to come here and I'll fix the little spell on the bus. You'll be able to walk out."

Cody knew somehow, she just knew in her bones, that this demon was being truthful. She was really giving Cody a chance to be there, torture free, but as good a saleswoman as she was, Hell just wasn't where she wanted to be. "Thank you, but I'm good, blondie."

"Aren't you feisty," she replied back with a wink.

The bus driver frowned at the interaction and sped off into the night. He shouted out the window as he pulled away from Hell. "No sales pitches. Those are the rules, Michelle."

"Fuck you, Arch-angel," the clip-board demon yelled back to the bus driver.

In a blink of an eye the bus stopped again. *Were Heaven and Hell really that close together? Creepy.* A bright light filled the whole bus and a calm came over everyone. Even the people in the creepier part of the bus seemed happy. The blood magically faded from their faces and they looked like they did when they were alive. Even Cody's cuts magically vanished. *How strange and amazing at the same time.*

The bus driver's voice was softer this time as he announced where they were, "Heaven. We've reached Heaven."

The bus driver leaned over the steering wheel and grabbed his clipboard reading off the names of the few people allowed to get off. "If you're ready, please leave the bus. Check your surroundings and make sure to take all your personal belongings with you."

Cody didn't want to spend an eternity on a bus. That was not her idea of a fun afterlife. But was she really dead?

Cody closed her eyes -- now was the last chance to remember. She blocked out everything else, the people, the light, the choice she'd have to make and only focused on her memory. She saw burning metal and heard a loud crash. It sounded close to her. Then she saw a blinding light and heard a car horn go off. That should have been a warning to pay closer attention to the road. She was tired, driving all night to make it back to her university. The truck was swerving down the highway, a rock came off the back of it and broke her windshield narrowly missing her head. That should have been yet another warning to stop the car and get out. *Hindsight's 20/20.*

Cody remembered the glass breaking on the passenger side window as the truck came crashing into her. She screamed as glass went everywhere. The last thing she remembered was a flashlight shining into her eyes as the EMS workers tried to save her. All the sensations she remembered, she experienced, the shadows chasing her, the smashed windshield, the rock that a shadow seemingly threw, the blinding light, they were all clues that her brain was trying to give her, so she could figure out what had happened. Cody knew she was dead now and all because of a truck. *Wow. How ignominious.* Cody felt sad and angry for a moment before the light made her calm again. *Strange how the light did that.* It was making her feel peaceful and wiping away all trace of negative emotion.

The choice was clear. As scary as it is to go into the unknown, waiting years or centuries on a bus wasn't a great alternative. But that girl, that petrified girl she saw on the freaky side, she couldn't leave her. Cody noticed how anxious the girl looked to get out when her name was called by the bus driver. Maybe majoring in social work would actually pay off. She moved to the back of the bus and sat next to the girl, ignoring the growl from the monster next to her.

Cody knew she only had a few minutes here so there was no point in sugar coating anything. Being blunt was the only way to go. "I'm Cody and I'm getting off this bus. I'd like to take you with me. What's keeping you here?"

"I can't I--," the girl insisted, scared, her voice trembling.

"You don't belong here. Let me free you from this man. All you have to do is take my hand. He can't stop you from leaving. He can't leave. This is your choice, your moment to be free." Cody held out her hand and smiled warmly at the girl.

"But- -," the girl started to say, confused. *It couldn't be that easy, could it?*

"He has no power over you. You have been stuck here for who knows how long. It's time to get off, don't you think? You've given him enough of your years."

The couple held hands as they walked out into the light smiling back at Cody.

"What about the others?" the girl inquired.

"They're not ready yet. They'll get off when they are."

The girl smiled shyly at Cody. She slowly stood up and nervously took Cody's hand. They both ignored the wails and growls and threats from the monster behind them. The girl was no longer tied to him. They slowly exited the bus holding hands as a bright light engulfed them.

They both closed their eyes and when they opened them, they found themselves in a large forest. The sun was out, birds were chirping, and beyond the white gates in front of them, Cody heard laughter.

A red-haired woman approached them seemingly from nowhere. Her voice was soothing and her smile genuine. "Welcome to Heaven, ladies," she announced. "Follow me and I'll show you around."

———————

FIVE

Never Fear, Bobo's Here

B obo must have been standing outside the bank for half the day waiting for just the right customers to come along. He made sure to hide in the bushes -- no sense in freaking anyone out just yet. He rather liked having the element of surprise.

But after all this time waiting, Bobo was starting to lose hope and wondered if he should just call it quits. He had figured that families would go to this bank. I mean it was the only bank for miles, a 24-hour bank and it was the weekend. But, alas, there were no families and more important, no children.

For the past five hours, only balding men in their late thirties and elderly women came and went. This was so frustrating, and Bobo was starving. When a family finally showed up, he hoped he would still have his wits about him, sometimes the hunger made him a little crazy.

Bobo impatiently tapped his giant clown shoe on the cement parking lot. He was thinking of murder and remembering his last kill in the hope that he could stave off boredom. So far it wasn't working.

He cautiously glanced over at the tellers and customers in the bank across the parking lot. The bank had huge glass windows and he was at the perfect vantage point to see every person in the bank. In the morning, when he arrived here, he studied the humans inside busying themselves with papers and frenzied movements. He didn't understand what they did but they looked nervous and committed to their boring little existences.

He tried to will a family into existence with no luck. He did get a death glare from an old woman who happened to park her car right next to him. *Just his luck.* He might be an immortal being but that look sure did give him chills. He refrained from staring back at her with red eyes, content to just go on with his business until she muttered something unsatisfactory about him. He simply gave her the creepiest smile known to man. The old woman literally ran into the bank.

You had to love humans and their hubris. An old woman, a human judging him? He found that hilarious really. All bark and no bite … unlike him. This small interaction tempered his mood a bit and distracted him so by the time he noticed the family, they were already on the line, with only three people ahead of them.

Of all the days for the bank to be competent, today was not the day. Soon the family would be gone, away from this deserted bank off the highway. Away from him into their safe, cozy house with peaceful dreams. Away from his hungry stares and evil intent. No, no, that would not do. Not after waiting hours for them to appear. But what could he do? He couldn't simply run in there. That would be strangely comical and wouldn't send the right message. Fear was what Bobo wanted, not ridicule. It's rather frustrating sometimes being stuck in a clown vessel. He eats one child of a powerful witch and gets stuck as a clown forever. How unfair.

He was terrible at making split-second decisions. He agonized over decisions, but he didn't have time here to do that here. He had to make a decision quickly. He decided to at least get a little closer to the bank doors. Get a closer look at the family and then maybe get the little boy then or at least get his scent so Bobo could find him later. Maybe a little run was in order, though with his huge cerulean blue clown shoes, running might prove to be difficult.

Bobo hadn't calculated just how difficult until he was face down on the ground. A centuries-old being brought to the ground by shoes or rather his shoelaces. How ignominious. He actually hurt his chin and his costume was a little scratched and soiled. Bobo was a prideful being and not at all happy with his now dirty costume. He brushed himself off as best as he could, growling as he tried to fast walk, and not run, to the big glass double doors of the bank. He tripped about three more times, the last time when his white gloved hand was on the door handle. That was the only thing that saved him from falling on his ass. *Hey, you try running in those shoes. Not easy.* The family were already at a teller. The line went really fast today.

A young boy in his family's car, driving away from the bank, laughed at him. Bobo rolled his eyes that a human thought it wise to mock him and that he missed a child somehow. How did he not see the child in the bank? He was outside waiting for hours. How did he miss him? *Wow, was he horrible at what he did.* The clown lifted his head slowly and showed the boy his true form and the boy shrank back in abject horror. That made the clown happier. He could still scare kids, at least; he wasn't a total fuckup. Growling at himself, he focused on the family in the bank. He couldn't miss them. Why not grab the boy now instead of just watching him? Yeah, Bobo was too hungry to just watch anyway.

Bobo grabbed the door handle again victorious, only to fall forward hitting the glass hard. Stupid overly polished glass doors. Everyone in the bank looked at the door. He could feel their laughter. Growling deep in his throat, Bobo opened the door slowly and managed to get in. These peons would have to die. No one laughs at Bobo. NO ONE!

Bobo took a couple of seconds to recover. He wasn't used to running after people or being ridiculed and judged so damn often. When he recovered, the family was gone, no longer at the teller. *Just his luck.* He facepalmed and got some of the white face makeup on his gloved hand. *"You've got to be kidding me. Seriously?! Wow. I do suck. After 300 years of doing this, I suck! Maybe I'm just having a bad day? Or maybe I really am an idiot. Maybe my brother's right. The witch really messed me up. Learned my lesson though. Don't eat the progeny of witches!"*

Groaning, the clown walked slowly to the back door and swung it open, hoping to catch the family before they drove off. He saw the family in the parking lot. He had to stop them somehow. He took out a whoopee cushion from his giant clown pants. You'd be surprised how many things he had in there. He threw it in the air to the boy. Or rather he tried. It stopped midway and slammed into a car making an awkwardly loud sound midway between a snore and a dying duck. *I can't even throw right!* The boy was intrigued. I mean who doesn't like whoopee cushions. He picked it up eyeing the clown and smiled. *A creepy clown smiles and gives you something and you accept it? What is his mother teaching him? And even better his mother didn't notice. Maybe my luck is looking up?* This family would be fun, Bobo was sure of it.

The security guard started yelling at him, ordering him to listen to him. *The gale of some people.* The people at the bank started talked, murmuring about him. He hated people talking about him, they should fear him, period. No other talk about himself would do.

The security guard started yelling at him again. *Humans always thinking they own the world.* Bobo was going to have to shut this guy up. The clown slowly turned around to look at the man in front of him. The cop was well over his prime, fat and slow, real slow, judging by the time it took him to get his gun out. The uniform was tight on him, must have gained weight. It was also old and had faded spots on it. The cop was balding and had sun spots on his arms. This was humanity's protector? Or at least the humans in here? This putrid excuse for a human? Hadn't Bobo suffered enough?

The clown sighed at the display of violence. The security guard kept yelling something. What? Bobo couldn't be sure. He had stopped listening because it didn't matter what the strange human said, Bobo does what he wants when he wants. He is above reproach from humans.

The clown smiled and moved forward, walking up to the security guard. The guard fired, and the bullet hit the clown in the heart but got absorbed into his body. The clown lifted his hand up and flung the man clear across the room. "Wait your turn, silly boy," the clown stated with contempt. He walked into the bank deciding that minute to kill everyone for insulting him. He had to blame someone for his bad day -- why not them? They laughed at him after all. Laughing would be the last thing they did.

The squeak of his clown shoes on the linoleum floor made his appearance less than daunting but oh well. He literally couldn't take them off.

"Attention everyone at the bank. You all look so stressed and angry lately. I have something to cheer everyone up. I am a clown after all," Bobo announced in an overly cherry tone. He took a large balloon out of his pants that seemed to self-inflate before everyone's eyes.

Several customers tried to leave. Bobo simply shook his finger at them. *Naughty humans thinking they could outsmart the amazing, clever Bobo the clown.* He had locked the doors and windows, seconds ago with his mind. When he plans to kill, he does it with military precision. It's just up to that point that he's a bumbling idiot.

One brave little human pulled the alarm. Bobo was aware of that fact, but it didn't matter. By the time help arrived, everyone would be dead. The balloon drifted up to the ceiling, it would only be a matter of seconds now. Bobo bowed to his audience, excited for them to see his new trick.

"Enjoy," he said with a wide, inhuman smile on his face.

Bobo walked over to the cop and picked him up by his shirt collar. The man was still a bit groggy, his limbs protesting the harsh, rough way the clown held him. The clown showed him what he could of his true form. His eyes were the eyes of a rotting skeleton with a glowing red center to them. His mouth was wider than any animal's and stretched from ear to ear. His teeth were sharp, and several had blood stains on them. He couldn't transform the rest of the way because of that damn witch and he couldn't stay in this conceivably scarier visage for more than for a few seconds. But humans were a weak and frightened species. A few seconds was all he needed. Bobo touched the cop, who was frightened stiff just by Bobo's true face, and transferred a large amount of pain, more pain than any human could withstand, into the cop's mind killing him in a matter of seconds.

The cop's death left the clown hollow. Bobo didn't plan on

killing him, didn't want to, but he refused to let humans talk to him and fire at him like this one did. It was a matter of principle, nothing more. He didn't eat the man's soul. Adult souls had a nasty, pungent taste to them that he never got used to. Children's souls were sweet, delicate, and creamy. The people in the bank … he would enjoy their deaths. Revenge was always fun.

As if to commemorate an adult kill, which hadn't happened for Bobo in quite some time, the balloon popped and laughing gas came pouring out. The clown walked out the back door smiling as he heard the last laugh of everyone in that bank. Screams were a delicacy to him but laughs brought him a strange sense of joy. Bobo closed his eyes and relished their deaths before walking out to find the boy. Sirens wailed off in the distance though it was clearly too late.

The clown closed his eyes and arrived immediately at the boy's house. Since the boy had accepted the gift, it unknowingly created a mind meld so Bobo would be able to find him. Now, where was the boy's bedroom? He was drawn by muffled voices. He caught the end of a conversation, but it sounded as if the boy were afraid of what was under his bed. His silly mother told him there was no such thing as monsters. You have to love parents -- they make it so easy for monsters to prey on children since they're told they don't exist. The child *should* be afraid of what's under the bed. The child only seemed half convinced of what his mother told him. *Clever boy.* Ironic that he picked a child with night terrors. Oh, he'd show the child what a night terror really was, just you wait. The boy's mother kissed him and left the child alone in darkness. The perfect environment for Bobo to slip under the bed and wait for the right moment.

The clown bided his time waiting about an hour before he slowly slithered out from under the bed. He wanted to be sure mother dearest and the child were both asleep. The fear was more pungent if the child suddenly woke up. He didn't like killing adults if he didn't have to -- they were such a bother. And killing adults for him meant coming up with clever deaths, otherwise it was just banal, and it looked like he couldn't handle the situation. But if he creatively killed adults he seemed like a maverick to his kind, a clever psychopath and not an incompetent moron who simply couldn't control the situation. Others of his kind never ever killed parents, they never had, they were *that* good. They could get in and get out undetected. He was never that lucky.

Bobo licked his lips and leaned over the boy going in for the kill, finally. There was no mother in sight, maybe he was lucky today. That thought was dashed when the door swung open dramatically and loudly, slamming against the wall.

The mother came into the room smirking at Bobo, holding a sword. Bobo gulped. Did this human really know what could kill him? That would mean she knew what he was, which should be impossible unless yet again, the child wasn't human. *Fuck.*

The mother's intense, angry gaze softened when she looked over at her son. "It's okay, honey, run into the kitchen. You're safe. It's going to be okay. Let mommy handle this, okay?"

The boy didn't need to be told twice. He bolted out of there in seconds. When she was sure her son was out of earshot, she spoke to the clown freely.

"You know, for a demon, you really are an idiot," the mother proclaimed. "I knew you gave him the toy. You're about as subtle as a tornado. I heard the sound as it fell on the car; the whole exchange was heavy handed and obvious. And I do read the papers. Killing two children in the same neighborhood? Hello! Monster 101! Change towns after a kill. People start putting two and two together otherwise."

"What are you?" the clown inquired fearfully. This mother was the first in a long life to make him feel afraid and Bobo didn't like it one bit.

"Your worst nightmare," she mocked. "I know how to kill you. But what or who I am is of no importance. Did you really think I would just leave him unattended, so you could eat his soul? Did the other mothers do that?"

"Mothers sleep during the night," Bobo replied confused.

"I'm a vampire. I don't sleep. Do your homework," she spat in disgust.

"How was I supposed to know?" Bobo cried out.

"Monster to monster? You follow the family first, suss them out, get their routine, see what they do, see if the parents are monsters. My husband is a werewolf, by the way. Careful with the volume of your voice. Wouldn't want to wake him up. He'd eat you alive. Hmm…interesting thought. I always wondered how demon tastes."

Bobo tried to use his powers on the mother but noticed the hex bags and the sigils on the walls of her son's room. She was prepared. He hadn't seen them before, too intent on the boy.

"You're not getting his soul and you're not killing any more children. Me and my husband do kill, but we kill the villains, the dregs of society like yourself. I could make you into a pancake for tomorrow. Or maybe I'll kill you. It would be beneath me to eat you."

The clown was wracking his brains and literally pulling everything out of his pants to try and destroy her. He suddenly felt a whoosh of air and then saw her coming toward him with a sword, a millisecond later and his head was on the floor.

Her husband came running in. "Are you OK, honey? Tyler is a nervous, blubbering mess in the kitchen."

"He's seven, Brennan. Relax. He'll grow into being a werewolf. We had a demon problem."

"The damn clown! It was a Kagedra demon?"

"Yep. He lost his head."

Brennan frowned at his wife's matter-of-tone. "Haven't seen those in a long time. We're going to have to leave, you know."

"Yep. Traveling again it is, you're quite right, darling. Explaining this and why my child survived will be hard. People will look at our family closely, too closely, better to just disappear. Become someone else."

"I'll tell Tyler and pack us up a few snacks."

"I'll pack up," she offered.

They kissed briefly before doing their set tasks, angry that a demonic clown kicked them out of town.

Bobo didn't stand a chance. Mothers are more powerful than any evil. Not to mention a vampire mother.

R.I.P. dear Bobo the clown.

SIX

Welcome to Hell Inc.

Mondays are the bane of everyone's existence, the start of a long work week. Gary stumbled out of bed cursing his lot in life which was to work as some faceless, unimportant peon in a giant uncaring corporation. When he was in school, he had an idea that he'd become some kind of artist, but life has a way of forcing you to make more practical financial decisions. Sighing dramatically, he exited his barely furnished, cramped apartment and traveled an hour on a smelly, packed train to get to work.

Every day Gary would wave at the security guard and every day the guard was suspicious of Gary, thinking him an intruder. He would scowl and frown at the simple wave, demanding some ID. Gary happily obliged, but the guard never offered any apologizes for mistaking him for a trespasser. He simply shrugged apathetically. Gary had worked here at the Firm going on fifteen years. It would be nice if someone remembered him but that was never the case. Gary's confidence would deflate at that point and he'd always bow his head as he walked over to the elevators to face even more scorn.

The elevator in the morning was always packed with people. They'd squish him as if they couldn't see he was standing there. It was as if he were invisible. He had to shove people out of the way to even get out the door and then was called "rude." He always said, "Excuse me," three times and they never moved. It was their fault, not his, but he was the kind of guy who was only too happy to put the blame on himself. He was the fuckup, the sad sack, the boring, plain, nobody, and he knew that nothing he did would ever get anyone to see him differently.

He got to his cubicle and sat down quickly, relieved that the journey was done. Now he could just get to work. No other human interaction was needed. The monotony of his day, the cruelty of his coworkers, coupled with the institutional white walls and blackout curtains made it feel like he was working in Hell. Little did he know that soon he would be able to compare the differences.

He walked like a zombie over to the break room to grab some coffee. He longed for a girlfriend, and had one in college, a beautiful girl way out of his league, whom he treasured very much. Somehow, they became distant or someone changed, or maybe they wanted different things. Everything crumbled so fast he couldn't be sure *exactly* what caused it. He should have fought harder to keep her but like everything in his life, he just let it go. Any resistance, any scorn and he just let go; he took it and retreated into himself. He never fought back, never spoke up; he really didn't see the point. It was easier to stay quiet and wait until it was over. He was a great employee, hardly ever called in sick, and could work any day. Had no family to speak of. He was almost always the one they asked to stay late and work overtime on weekends.

Gary smiled when he drank his coffee. He loved the taste and it gave him a justifiable reason for a break. He sometimes had as many as seven cups of coffee, mostly just for a chance to breathe. He was looking at the floor memorizing the pattern of the carpet when a man stepped in front of him. A man that was acknowledging him. He looked all around him. Was this a mistake? He looked over at the man to see he was wearing a uniform and was holding what looked like a package. A courier for him? Who would be sending him a package much less talking to him?

"Are you Gary Frontini."

He stared at the courier intently trying to gauge whether this was a joke. After a beat he saw the impatience on the man's face.

"Look, I got a couple of deliveries so – uh, are you-."

"Yes, it's me. I'm Gary."

"Great, you got a package. Please sign here," he said matter-of-factly but tipped his hat to Gary all the same. His voice sounded deep, but he looked no older than 16. *Shouldn't he be in school?*

Gary was in a daze as he signed the paper mechanically, utterly confused as to who would be sending him anything. No one even knew where he worked. He had no friends or family to speak of.

"Open it when you're alone," the courier demanded. Then he offered Gary a haunting smile before he turned and made his way down the hall. The whole exchange was rather weird to Gary who never had any excitement in his life. He was excited to see what this package was and figure out this little mystery. He supposed that sometimes Mondays *could* be interesting.

As the courier walked away, his shoes seemed to make a strange echo. But where could the echo come from? Office buildings aren't places where echoes are created. Are the shoes special?

Gary had a mind to ask him who sent the package and so turned around to see where the courier was now. The man moved rather quickly and was almost at the door when he suddenly disappeared. There was no other way to describe it. One minute the courier was there and the next, he was gone. Like the man teleported somewhere but that's crazy.

Gary shook his head shifting focus from the strange disappearing courier to the package in his hands. What a curious little package it was. As he walked the long way back to his cubicle, he felt he was being watched. He turned around to see who was staring at him, but everyone's eyes were on their own work. The only one even vaguely glancing at him was the boss's cat. And a tabby couldn't be the cause, right? That's ludicrous. The feeling of being watched didn't leave him as he started to open it, needing to find out what this was all about. A strange hissing sound of paper and plastic filled the air as he finally got the box open. No one looked his way which was awfully strange given how loud the sound was. Were they all deaf? Shrugging at the weirdness of this particular Monday, Gary slowly looked down into the cavernous package and simply saw papers and a small business card. How very strange. It read:

> Hell Inc.
> Your wish is our desire
> Satisfied Customers since 1643
> CEO: The Devil
> Creative Director: Lilith

On the back was a phone number. Gary honestly thought it was a joke, wouldn't you? His reasoning was that there was no such thing as Hell or the Devil. He had a mind to throw the card out, but something urged him to keep reading, to find out more.

There were a couple of pieces of parchment paper with instructions of some sort and his name was on the top.

It read:

Hello Gary Frontini,

You have been selected by our Master for a rare gift. If you choose to accept the offer, please return the sheet attached to the address on the back of this paper. Our Master is prepared to offer you anything for the low price of your soul. That's right, human, anything. The only limit is your own imagination! This is a very lucrative offer and as with most offers, it comes with a time limit. You have 48 hours to decide whether you'd like to take us up on the offer. No more being a peon in a company that couldn't care less about you. No more being ignored and forgotten. You can have everything you desire. All you have to do is ask. You're the only thing stopping you from having the life you deserve.

So that we can help you more effectively and tailor your wish more closely to your specific taste, please answer a few questions and a demon representative will get back right back to you as soon as possible.

Thank you for taking the time to fill this out. We want only happy customers. We are confident you will enjoy your wish. We ask, though, that you be sure about your decision to hire us since once hired, there is no firing us or running away. By filling this out, signing it, and sending it to us, you are entering into a legal contract from which there is no way out.

If you have any questions or require immediate assistance or just want to speak to a representative before signing, the toll-free number is on the back of our business card. We are open 24 hours, 7 days a week. Thank you for choosing Hell Inc. to make your dreams come true.

Required Information:

Your name:
Your age:
Your family life/love life:
Your reasons for choosing Hell Inc.:
Your wish/wishes:
Your phobias/fears:
Your problems:
Your dreams:
What makes you happy:
What makes you sad:
What do you want to accomplish on earth:

Your Signature _____

Today's Date _____

Hell Inc
Your desire is our business
Satisfied Customers since
1643

Standard Soul Contract for Gary Frontini

I, _____ being of sound mind and body do hereby relinquish all ownership rights and privileges associated with this soul that is mine and mine alone to be dispensed with as this contact details. By signing this contract, I am giving my soul to Satan in return for the aforementioned wishes. If the wishes are vague, it is up to the demon representative or Satan himself to verify with you, Gary Frontini, what exactly you are looking for.

I, _____ will in no way, shape or form ever attempt to appeal the conditions and stipulations of this contract to what would be considered a higher authority and/or power over the realm of Hell, and/or the realm of Earth and or any other realm, plane, dimension or other unspecified construct of existence or celestial body within the confines of this or any other Universe.

Any dispute of other matters in question arising out of, or relating to, the formation, interpretation, performance, or breach of this contract, whether such dispute arises before or after the execution of this contract shall be voided and resolved by the simple understanding that the soul bearer has no further or prior claims upon said soul after signing this contract.

At the time of your death, you will become an employee of Hell Inc. in a position decided upon by Satan himself. You will not be able choose your position in Hell Inc once dead. Your death will not be hastened by the Devil. You will die when you are meant to die, how you are meant to die. Fate will determine the exact when and how. It is possible that you may work for Hell Inc. when you are a human. Those decisions are left up to the discretion of the CEO of Hell Inc., the Devil.

Hell Inc. is a demonic corporation. Its subsidiaries include; "Wishes Inc.," "Demonic Wishes Inc.," "Hellfire Studios," "News from Hell" (The only newspaper from Hell), the rock band, "Acolytes of the Devil," the nightclub, "Death Incarnate," and the restaurant, "Hellfire and Brimstone." All of the businesses listed above are owned by Satan and his partner, Lilith, and are places the deceased may work.

I understand that by signing this contract I am agreeing to the stipulations contained herein.

_____
Soul Bearer/the Wisher

_____

Date

_____

The Devil, CEO of Hell Inc.

_____

Date

_____

Demonic Representative

_____

Date

_____

Lilith, the Creative Director of Hell Inc.

_____

Date

Gary must have stared at the paper long enough to memorize every word. The legal document was a nice touch but no matter how nicely it phrased everything, it couldn't be real, could it? Gary thought not and after a long day of work and banal data entry, he shuffled home same as usual. The contract and Hell Inc. swirling around in his mind.

He used the time on the train to really think about the offer. It could be an elaborate prank from the legal department. Yeah, punk the nobody. It's possible but it could also be the truth. *"Now might be the time to suspend disbelief,"* he mused. *If it's true, this is my only change to change my lot in life. There's no harm in signing on the dotted line, right? Who needs a soul anyway? Maybe it's like an appendix."*

Required Information

Your name: Gary Frontini
Your age: 42
Your family life/love life:
Your reasons for choosing Hell Inc.:
Your wish/wishes: I want to be respected, loved, wealthy and famous doing an important job. Oooh and maybe even have some powers.
Your phobias/fears: Insects and claustrophobia
Your problems:
Your dreams:
What makes you happy:
What makes you sad: Being ignored, alone and unappreciated
What do you want to accomplish on earth:

Your Signature _____

Today's Date _____

Gary filled out a few questions immediately but figured if he was really going to do this, he wanted to think about it, sleep on it even, and see if he still thought this was a good idea in the morning. They did say he had 48 hours.

Gary slept peacefully but the decision was weighing on his mind. He woke up at 2 AM and decided to finish the form and sign his name. He hated his life and literally had nothing to lose, only gain, or so he thought. Why not sign it? His dreams had been quite insistent that it was a good idea. He saw himself in his dream having everything he desperately wanted. Had the Devil invaded his dreams or was Gary tempting himself? Who knows, but from the second Gary woke up, he knew that he had to sign. He'd worry about mailing off the documents in the morning but at least he signed. He knew he made the right decision and went back to bed with a smile on his face. He was finally getting his life together. And soon he'd wake up to a better one.

The Devil smiled, knowing instantly the exact moment Gary signed. He could just feel it. The small soul tracker he had on his desk slowly added one more to his soul tally for the day, the numbers glaring at him in red. He smiled before he teleported himself to Gary's apartment to watch the man sleep. A lot could be discovered by watching a man sleep and by rifling through his belongings.

The second the Devil arrived, he frowned at the abyssal apartment. The place was barely furnished. The Devil rolled his eyes dramatically.

Gary seemed to be a sound sleeper and didn't have any nightmares or at least wasn't having one now. A curious little fact for such a put-upon man. Apparently, he didn't dwell too much on negativity. He endured and moved on. Good to know. The Devil walked around the room again before he took out the surveillance videos Lilith was able to secure. Now was as good a time as any to review Gary's work life. He frowned at Gary's co-workers. It all became quite clear why this man would sign so quickly. He didn't even call the hotline; no communication at all. They almost always do. Humans are a rather curious race. Lilith was right in her briefing; this man had nothing to lose.

The Devil had felt this man's longing so intensely that he came to personally take care of the deal. He looked over the form and smiled at how much the man asked for. Gary found the Devil in a good mood and he might just give him everything he wanted, of course not exactly how he wanted it, but that's the whole thing about deals and wishes, isn't it? The Devil took the forms and signed his name on the dotted line. He didn't want to frighten the poor man, no need to wake him up just yet. So the Devil chose to sit in Gary's comfy, rocking chair with a plush pillow on the seat. Curious that there was a rocking chair with a cushion on it and little else in the room.

At some point close to sunrise, the boss's cat suddenly appeared in the Devil's lap. The Devil chuckled as he pet her, happy when she purred at his touch.

"You did well, darling, as you always do. We really do make a wonderful team."

The cat transformed into a voluptuous woman, with amble breasts and curves that would drive any man wild. She stood up from his lap stark naked. She glanced down his figure taking in his instant erection.

"Glad to know I've still got it. And yes, you and I, dear, are forever. Best partners in the history of time."

The Devil pulled her close, his strong arms winding around her back holding her to him. He gently tilted her head up with his left hand before pressing his lips to hers. He could honestly stand here forever just like this, kissing her and making love to her for all eternity. They were both busy people, running Hell together. She had the creative side, he the day-to-day, and sometimes it was a while until they had time to themselves. They never hesitated to sneak in a kiss or two. And there was always passion, always fire between them. They only had eyes for each other since the beginning of time. They were, well, "soulmates," though neither of them had souls.

In seconds, the kiss turned passionate. She moaned into the kiss ready to submit to her master completely. Her arms wound around his neck to keep him there. Her fingers grabbed his hair for leverage.

He moaned as she gently tugged on his hair. In response, he did what he always did, nibbled on her bottom lip which never failed to make her gasp. He chuckled into the kiss as his tongue dove into hers, fighting for dominance and winning easily. He explored her mouth, reacquainting himself with it as he toyed with her tongue. They didn't need to breathe so they could stay here for hours, and he wished he could. but their recent mark, in their rather long con, named Gary, would soon awaken. The sight of the Devil himself would cause quite a stir but lip locking with his beloved would be more jarring than necessary.

Slowly he stepped back from Lilith. She gave him a small pout in response.

"Are you sure about this one?" Lilith inquired.

"I sure hope so, my beloved. I can't imagine that it was very much fun for you to be a cat for two weeks just to get intel on him. I am quite sure he will make a good addition and as you know, it's so much more fun to corrupt a good man into doing evil than to simply give him what he wants and later on make him a demon. He's so corruptible, so full of self-pity, he's begging for it. And it's been a while since I got to corrupt anyone. I'm owed one."

Lilith shrugged before replying, "I'm just happy this con will be over. I'm starting to act like a cat."

"Now there's a roleplay for you."

"Maybe after you close this deal, sir," Lilith teased knowing the Devil had a huge ego as well as a huge package and he always liked to be the dominant partner. Lilith, as much as she liked to dominate, loved to submit to him more. Lilith knew the word "sir" made him absolutely crazy. She watched as his eyes turned darker and he growled, hating to be teased when he should be working. She winked at him, unfazed by the growl. She was never one for playing by the rules, not all the time at least. She shapeshifted back into a cat and with a meow teleported to Gary boss's apartment, to see if there was any more intel to be had.

A few minutes later, a groggy, listless Gary woke from his slumber to find a large shadow in the corner of his room on his rocking chair. He froze in bed, the blanket in his hand. He didn't even go for a weapon.

The Devil smiled at him. His corruption would be so much fun to watch.

"Well, hello there, Gary. You're quickly becoming a person of interest. I don't usually make house calls.

Gary having just woken up, desperately tried to get his bearings and figure out what the hell was going on. The Devil's voice was deep but had a jovial tone to it as if he were conversing with a friend. He slowly stepped out of the shadows so that Gary could get a look at him.

The Devil was classically handsome like someone from an old movie. He oozed power and danger. There was a dark glint in his eye even though he was smiling. You could tell the smile wasn't entirely sincere. The Devil walked with purpose as he strolled over to a fearful Gary who was still frozen in bed. The Devil had his hands in his pockets as he observed the man in bed. He raised his eyebrows when he saw Gary was wearing superhero pajamas. Gary ignored the look and instead focused on the fact that a strange man was in his room. A man who wore a faded classic rock T-shirt with tailored woolen pants, mixed with vintage wingtip shoes. *Talk about a creative dresser.*

"You're…. you…"

"Oh, my boy. Please tell me I haven't wasted my time. You still don't know who I am? Really? Come now, have a little think. It involves a contract?"

"The Devil, you're the Devil?!"

The Devil frowned. This one would be fun, but he could be so banal and stupid sometimes. He signs on the dotted line and boom a strange man appears and he can't put it together? And even worse, this job prevented the Devil from having sex with Lilith. Two weeks with only heavy petting and a few kisses. The Devil was beyond sexually frustrated, so this man had better be worth it. Deciding to cut him some slack, because as they say, you catch more flies with honey than vinegar, the Devil went from frustrated to theatrical in one fell swoop.

He outstretched his arms and bowed in front of Gary. His voice changed into an announcer's voice and his hand gestures were bigger, grander.

"The one and only ruler of Hell at your service, for the moment that is. We have so much to discuss, no? Aren't you a needy little boy? I signed the forms by the way. You were asking for a lot but kid, you got potential. Yeah, those morons at your old job couldn't see it but I can. Come on now, follow me," the Devil said beckoning Gary to get out of the bed.

A couple of seconds later, they arrived at what looked like an underground facility. The outside looked strangely like an underground bunker. There was a keypad, but the Devil was so quick to punch in numbers that Gary couldn't tell what the code was. *There went thoughts of escape.* The door opened, leading into an empty, dilapidated warehouse. Gary followed the Devil looking around at the level of decay he found himself in. Was the Devil taking him here to kill him?

As if the Devil could read his mind, which he could, he replied, "Would I really go to all this trouble if I wanted you dead? Please, give me some credit, Gary."

He stopped abruptly at a hallway, that curiously held a gargoyle, next to what was left of a door. The hinges were still there and there a doorway but no door, just utter darkness, darkness that seemed to be alive. There were shapes forming and things slithering in it.

"Hello, old friend. Ticket for two please. The express to Hell," he joked.

The Gargoyle came alive and licked its master before spitting out two tickets. A man came out of the darkness, a train conductor it seemed, one dressed in period clothing from the 40's. The man quickly took the two tickets and bowed to the Devil. In the blink of an eye, Gary and the Devil found themselves in a huge compartment, on a period train speeding off to Hell, going way too fast for Gary's comfort.

"Usually people that come here via the ferryman are already dead. You, my good boy, are the exception but don't worry, everyone knows you're alive and I don't wish to call my chits in early. No need to be afraid. Hell will be good to you and this is part of your wish. Everything will soon be clear but for the love of everything evil can you please get your shit together and act like a man! You're making me look bad. Calm the fuck down. You're not dying. The train isn't going to crash. It has to go fast, otherwise we'd be here for years."

Gary's fearful gaze turned to the Devil who met him with a

stern look, like a scolding father. Gary swallowed awkwardly and decided to read the brochure about Hell instead.

In a matter of minutes, they were in Hell and the train doors were opening. Lilith was there to greet them. The second the Devil saw her, his gaze turned heated and his eyes were completely black with desire.

"Down boy," Lilith whispered in his ear.

"No one tells me what to do."

"Oh no, I'll have to be punished," she teased with a wink.

The Devil subtly growled his approval and then raised his eyebrows pointedly.

"Straight to business now? No more sexy talk? You're giving a girl whiplash here," Lilith teased before sighing and losing all trace of playfulness. Her stance was rigid and her tone matter-of-fact. "I went over one last time in cat form to check the place out. There's no more intel to be had on Gary here. What I was able to gather before is all we have."

The Devil nodded and introduced Lilith to Gary. She stiffly shook his hand, not that he noticed.

"The Creative Director of Hell? What does that mean?" Gary asked not missing a beat.

Lilith chuckled before speaking. "What a curious one he is. The long and short of it is that he deals with the business side and I do the cons, gather intel, tempt people, and generally work behind the scenes. I also decide on the décor and appearance of Hell from century to century. We went through several makeovers. I also work with press, make ads, set up interviews with the Devil and I make commercials and informercials about Hell, etc."

"That sounds like a lot."

"It is Gary. Well, I don't want to hold you two up any longer. I'll leave you boys to it. Bye now."

The Devil watched her go, sending all sorts of naughty images her way to tease her back, before snapping Gary and himself onto the main floor.

Gary saw rows of cubicles, but they weren't like any cubicles he'd ever seen. These were huge and more like mini rooms. They each had a comfy ergonomic leather chair in front of a huge computer; a shower, bathroom, a small kitchen, a couch, a bed, a fridge, and a mini library. It was like a home away from home. All the comforts of home while you toil away at work. What an interesting concept.

Off in the distance Gary could see a huge mall with movie theaters; an arcade, a whole lot of shopping, and a few restaurants and bars. It was like an underground city over here. There was even an apartment complex and a hotel chain. The windows in each cubicle were different. Apparently, the shape of the window and the view could be changed with a click of a button.

Gary was so utterly confused not only about how his wish had taken him here but that this was what Hell really looked like. He was getting nervous and having palpitations. All the Devil did was laugh.

"Dear boy, try to loosen up. Hell isn't a dreary place. It isn't fire and brimstone – well, it was at one point but Lilith, rightfully so, thought it needed a re-do. Hell went corporate. What do you think of this newest renovation?"

"It's a mini city and the rooms are --."

"Spacious. It *is* a city. Customer service is a hard job and I work hard to make sure my employees have a good work - life balance and enjoy their time working in Hell." The Devil scoffed at Gary, frustration evident in his tone, "Calm down Gary. I can hear your heart about to beat out of your chest. As I said before, you're safe here. No one would dare harm my new protégé.

"Why am I here?" Gary inquired fearfully.

"Right. Of course. I'm a bad host, forgive me. You're here because this will be your new job. As per your request, you're famous or will be. You're the only human here, everyone else is a demon, that's rock star status down here. And everyone already knows you. You're welcome here. You're wealthy because I pay very well. Up there, millionaires are businessmen but down here I know a business can't run right without customer service, so I pay handsomely. And I've arranged a coupling for you. She's a demon everyone wants, absolutely gorgeous but has a particular liking for gentler men, so I think you two would be great together. No more pining away for a woman. I spoke to her about it and she agreed. Go win your girl."

"She's okay with --."

"Elsie saw your picture, I spoke at length to her about you and she is anxious to meet you. She never really took to any of the demons around here, claiming they were too…what was her word, "caveman-esque." Yeah, she's eloquent that one," the Devil said with a smile.

"This isn't what I asked for."

"Isn't it? I've told you how this fits in with your wish, please tell me you were listening because I hate repeating myself. It's a pet peeve of mine. Now, I didn't mention the powers yet, but I gave you some. See, who says I'm not generous? You can read minds and project thoughts and images into people's minds. It won't work on me, Lilith or Elsie. We are big on consent here and mind powers muddy the waters a little."

Gary looked at him shocked.

"What? I'm evil, not tacky. I respect women thank you very much. Now, my dear boy I do believe you should get to work. Forgive me for not ushering you into this more smoothly, I'm a bit gruff or so I've been told. There's no way out and escaping will only make me mad, which trust me, you don't want to do. You have no choice, so you might as well choose to be happy."

Gary opened and closed his mouth shocked that he was stuck here. When he made the wish, he thought he'd work above on Earth, not in Hell. He wasn't a demon. It didn't work that way, right? The Devil didn't seem like a liar, but would demons accept him when humans couldn't? Could he really have a life here? It was crazy to consider. Gary wasn't a wicked man; he was a kind, gentle soul which was why the Devil was doing this, of course. But Gary wasn't sure he could do the task asked of him. He didn't want to hurt people. He also had no idea what was meant by customer service. Could he sell things for the Devil or whatever these people did? Could he damn others? Well he didn't have a choice, right?

The Devil left him to his own thoughts but found Gary frozen in the center of the room, a glazed look in his eyes, with just a twinge of sadness. That would not do.

"Gary, shape up and get with the program. I'll be right there in the corner office if you need me. I really would advise you to get to work. Your partner Trent will get you up to speed as I am a busy ruler. I'll be watching you, kid."

Gary slowly looked up at the Devil in front of him. He gulped when he saw how intensely he was looking at him. Gary shuffled over to his desk and sat down. Satisfied, for now at least that the human was sitting down, the Devil walked up to his corner office a level above the main floor of Hell Inc. His office was directly across from Gary's cubicle so he could keep an eye on his newest employee.

"The poor thing looks so lost, like a little puppy. He's adorable."

"Careful, my darling, I love you more than myself, but constantly teasing me isn't wise."

"Isn't it?" Lilith inquired as she slowly slid her dress down stepping out of it completely. She was stark naked, preferring never to wear underwear, it would just get ripped by the Devil anyway.

"You minx, you," he all but growled as he charged at her.

Gary looked at the phones and wondering what the hell his job was.

A cheerful, friendly demon thrust his hand in Gary's face. "Hey dude, I'm Trent. Man, it's good to meet you." Gary shook it tentatively. "Yeah good to meet you, too," Gary replied with barely any emotion behind it.

"Did the Chief tell you about the gig?"

Gary simply shook his head.

"Well, basically the gig is to field calls about Hell. There's an extensive answering machine service so we only get patched with people who have general questions. Demon deals get routed to the Deals Department, the Devil's calls get routed to Lilith who fields them for him, the Death Department deals with death related calls, etc."

Gary's mind was blown. It was way too much information, all at once. Trent smirked and simply called Hell's number letting Gary listen to the voice prompts. "Listen to this, it'll make everything clearer."

A chipper voice, too chipper even for an automated message, answered the phone after only one ring. As she spoke, there was classical music playing faintly in the background.

"Hello Monsieur, Madame. You have reached Hell Incorporated. All our representatives are currently helping other customers. We urge you to please stay on the line if you would like more information about our services and to speak to a customer service representative.

Press 1 for general information about Hell Inc. including our location and hours of operation. Press 2 to speak with a demon representative to make a contract for your soul. Press 3 to make a contract for something else. Press 4 if you're recently dead and want to know your options. Press 5 to work here as required by the contract for your soul. Press 6 to leave a message directly for Satan and he will answer you *if* he wants. Press 7 for Lilith, the Creative Director of Hell, to give any comments about the service. Press 8 for a tour of Hell. Please note we only allow children under 12 if they are accompanied by an adult. Press 9 for information about school faculty positions, government positions, positions in the entertainment industry and news reporter positions, in Hell and in the general population. Press 10 for billing. Please note that due to the heavy volume of calls, your wait time might exceed our 20-minute policy. Press 11 if you' re dying or afraid of dying and want to be turned into a vampire or demon. We'll send someone over right away. Press 12 to become a dealer and help gather souls. Press 13 to become a Wish Master or a Siren. Press 14 to live in an alternate universe. Press 0 Right now if you're a politician, police officer, FBI agent, or other high-ranking official and would like to know the perks of working for us. Press 15 if you'd like to join our mailing list to keep you updated on current sales, positions and services. All members get 10 percent off at Hell Inc., the online store. Press 16 for all online orders. Please have your order number ready. Press 17 for any HR-related questions including benefits, health care for loved ones and promotions. Please have your employee ID handy.

Thank you for calling us and remember, at Hell Inc. your desire is our business. This message will repeat."

"Isn't that a rocking intro? Lilith is genius! Damn, it's awesome to work here and you're so lucky, dude. I, like, applied and applied to be a customer service rep. They pay so damn well and it's a cushy job. And I heard you and Elsie might be dating. You sly dog! You're awesome. The first human *ever* to work here, lands the best job and now the most sought-after girl? You're gonna be a legend man, just you wait." Trent beams at Gary, feeling so lucky to have been paired with him. Gary was going places and hopefully he'd take Trent with him.

At first, Gary hated the job and what was required of him. Some phone calls were really trying. It's hard to answer the phone and convince people to sell their souls knowing what's waiting for them on the other side. It's so much easier not knowing, but *knowingly* damning people? That's hard. And sometimes, it was a young person with their whole life ahead of them wanting to sell their soul.

In the first few months, Gary's heart would beat wildly out of his chest and he would wring his hands whenever the phone rang. But Trent always knew just what to say to calm him down and sometimes he even took over for Gary if the case was giving him that much trouble. All the while the Devil and Lilith were watching, and Gary knew it.

Trent was a good choice for a friend. Gary was actually happy that the Devil paired them up. Trent was knowledgeable, even patient when Gary's conscience was weighing on him, supportive when he got emotional and he was the best at offering pointers and ways to make the Devil happy. The Devil and Lilith stared at the poor man day in and day out. He was constantly being observed and he guessed they were also listening to check that he was a good employee. He knew there was no other choice but to make them happy, to be good at his job, and that meant to make sure people sold their souls. After a while it got easier. He had no choice as the Devil said so why fight it, right?

"Oh, hello there. You sound young…Ah, 16. Well, you came to the right place, dear. You can have anything you want. You can spend the rest of your life having the kind of life you deserve. Who cares about souls and consequences. That's just details. What do you say, should I connect you with a demon representative?"

"Yeah. Thanks mister. I think I'm ready."

"Wonderful. Thanks for calling Hell Inc. Your desire is our business."

Everyone in the office welcomed him with open arms. They celebrated his birthday, got to know him, listened to his ideas in the board room meetings, hung out with him, checked in on him often during work hours, invited him to after-work parties and baby showers. They constantly made an effort to be a part of his life. They celebrated him like an actual, valid human being that deserves friends and recognition. He was a rock star here as the Devil had said he would be. Everyone was clamoring to be his friend and ask his advice. He went from a nobody with humans, to the coolest kid on the block with demons. And they were great to know. Demons get a bad rap, but these guys were funny, kind, sensitive and not at all what Gary thought they'd be.

The Devil had stopped observing him after a few months, but Gary didn't know it. He kept seeing those shadows in the dark suite above his cubicle and thought that the Devil was always watching. He thought he had no choice, he was part of the Firm now. He had to please the boss. In fact, the Devil had simply called a stand-in to stay in his office and watch Gary. Satan would do it himself, but he was a busy man and this way Gary would be motivated to do his best all the time.

As for Elise, she was gorgeous, and the second Gary saw her, he wanted her. He saw how the other men looked at her and the idea that he would get her, and not better-looking demons sent a thrill through his entire body. At first it was just fun to have her, a girl that was so beautiful and sweet. A girl that could have done so much better than him. But she showed him that she really cared for him. And over time, his feelings became genuine and he fell madly in love with her. They spent all their time together. Their first date was just a casual coffee in the mall on the main floor of Hell. But since that date they were inseparable. They went on three dates a week quickly progressing into a relationship. Their love was intense and passionate. She was so happy to find the sensitive, loving, good man she desperately wanted. And Gary was so happy to find a woman who could love him through and through. They were two peas in a pod, puzzle pieces that fit so well together.

Elsie smiled, and it lit up the room, one look at Gary was all it took. Gary had his misgivings about working here and the work could be difficult and trying, but he felt so accepted by his peers and he finally had love, real love.

Gary never thought his wish would go like this, but he enjoyed it and gradually forgot about what he was doing on the phone. He finally had everything he wanted. As he lay in bed, his arms around Elsie and her now round stomach, he realized that the Devil didn't only take his soul, he took his empathy and compassion, his very humanity. And the sad part is that Gary wouldn't have it any other way.

———————————————

SEVEN

<< Rewind >>

The house is crawling with ivy at every corner. The porch, once filled with happy memories, is now damp with last month's rain. The swing that used to dance in the wind, lies still now, covered in dirt and grime. The door is stained with peeling paint, and the mirror in the hallway has a film of dust over the glass. The old wooden floorboards creak with sorrow. The TV that once showed its inhabitants their favorite shows during a delicious home cooked meal is now long since forgotten. The sofa gives out puffs of dust whenever it is sat on. A once happy, loving home, is now a decrepit structure, a ghost of its former self.

Looking up at the relic, Jenny tried to think of the best way to woo her new clients into buying the house. She was tasked with selling this unsellable house and she wanted desperately to prove herself to her male cohort. She knew the stories about the house, of course, but some people liked the idea of a haunted house and restless spirits. Surely it wouldn't be that hard to sell.

"This is a great fixer-upper, a bargain just waiting for a couple like you. Of course, there's a lot of work to be done but you've got to see it as it will be one day when you let the sunlight in and arrange for granite counter tops in the kitchen and a skylight in the office. See the wood on the walls as it will look once you scrape it down. Believe me – at this price, it's a steal. Classic architecture with a youthful, artistic feel."

The couple chuckled and smiled at each thing she brought their attention to. They nodded their heads and moved around the quiet house, unaware of the ghosts that still lived here on a different plane of existence. The ghosts saw the house as the place once was, not dusty and broken, as Jenny and the new people saw it.

Eventually, the young couple agreed to sign all the papers, ready to move in and start renovations in a month. With a sigh of relief, Jenny closed the door, triumphant that she had been the one to sell this place. The boys would never get over it. As she drove away, the high beams on Jenny's car lit up the dark house. The ghosts who still lived there were temporarily blinded, but of course, the real estate woman paid them no mind as she sped off, leaving the house to its own devices.

Mary squinted at the bright lights of Jenny's car that seemed like sunlight streaming through the windows. To her, it was morning.

Mary's room was messy, but the carpet was of the richest red imaginable. Clothes cluttered every inch of the room. Elegant, sexy, summer dresses lined the floor. The rickety chest swayed by Mary's bed. Light pink sheets from her canopy bed blew in the wind. Books old and new lay wherever space was available. The fireplace sat untouched on the opposite wall next to a periwinkle blue armchair.

Mike's room on the other hand, was almost a counterpoint to Mary's. His was always immaculate. Everything had its place. Ivory closets with tuxes and tailored pants glittered in the sunlight. Books lined the walls in disciplined shelves. His bed lay in the center with dark gray silken sheets dancing in the breeze. The white tiles in the bathroom shined like a happy kid showing the dentist he had no cavities.

Downstairs in the kitchen nothing extra lay in the cabinets. Just enough to get by. Two lonely plates lay in the sink. The stove lay waiting to be used but the lady of the house, Mary, never used it. As she would put it, "I wouldn't want to get my hands dirty. What a horrid idea that is. We have people for that." At the moment, only the two of them were in the house.

Mike sat in the living room staring into the fire, letting the crackle of the embers relax him. He must have been staring at them for ages, willing himself to make a decision. In times like these when his conscience weighed heavily on him, his father's voice spoke to him. In life, his father always egged him on to do unspeakable things for the good of the family. This instance was no different. "You're such a weak and pathetic man. Why did I have to have such a weak son? I ask you to do *one* thing, one *simple* thing, and you can't even do that right? You can't possibly love her? What is there to love? No, silly boy you married her for her money and yet you can't kill her for it? Ridiculous. She isn't even that pretty to look at, but she does have money. We've gone this far. Listen, she's in the shower, she won't even know what hit her. Make your father proud. Live up to the family name."

"It's not my fault you drank and gambled away the money," Mike pointed out.

"Don't you dare talk to your father that way. I will not be disrespected in my own house! You want to be a pauper on the streets begging? Do you? Because if you don't help your family, that's what will happen. How cute! Are you resisting me out of love and morals? Love and morals are useless boy! Haven't I taught you anything? Love makes you weak, don't forget it! Money is power. Love is what you use to get both. Now make me proud!" his father yelled in his mind.

Mike made a sound like a wounded animal. He knew that he couldn't resist any longer. His hand grabbed the poker in the fireplace, tears streaming down his face. He couldn't disappoint his father.

He made sure to keep his footsteps quiet. The water from the shower was doing most of the work for him. Mary was singing again. She wasn't a great singer but just the fact that she felt so relaxed and happy killed him inside. She felt safe and loved with him and here he was about to kill her. He was her husband. How could he do this? He closed his eyes for a moment, his conscience begging him to reconsider this act. He swallowed loudly trying to fight his emotions. His feet kept creeping up the stairs, having a will all their own. It was as if his father was guiding him towards the master bathroom.

The water stopped suddenly, abruptly, just as Mike was halfway there. He placed the hand not holding the fireplace poker, on the horrid wallpaper in the hallway, right by the bathroom. He took several calming breaths to try to quell his racing heart.

Mary gracefully put only her toe on the cold tiles, wincing at the brutal chill that wracked her body from just the slightest touch on the unforgiving tile floor. Like ripping off a bandage, she suddenly put both feet down on the floor, taking a deep breath of air. Mary wrapped a fluffy crimson red towel around her body before slowly running her fingers through her wet and knotty long brown hair. She smiled with her head off to the side as she tried to unknot a particularly stubborn lock of hair. She was happy to greet the day.

Slowly, she walked up to the now foggy mirror, her feet now happily on the small, plush, red carpet in the corner of her bathroom. She attempted to put makeup on, though it was quite hard to see her face clearly in the mirror. Her motto was to always look her best, even when the plan for the day was just to lounge around with her husband.

Mike took careful steps towards the bathroom, hugging the wall all the way until he reached the doorway to their huge bathroom. He closed his eyes and raised his hands.

Mary thought she heard a creak from outside but dismissed it since Mike never woke up this early. She saw a shadow in the doorway through the fog on the mirror and immediately tensed. Who was there?

Mary turned around and saw Mike with a poker in his hands and a dead look in his eyes. Her face scrunched up in fear, staring horror-struck. She tried to scream but nothing came out. There was a squelching sound and the poker struck her, a confused look on her face as she slowly fell to the ground. Her now cold body matching the equally cold tile floor, a pool of blood coloring the bland white tiles.

Mike bit his lip, conflicted, apologetic, angry and calm all at the same time. "I-I- haaad to do it. Pleeeease understand. There was no other way," he begged her corpse to understand, in a voice that shook with emotion.

Mike went to the safe where she kept some of the money she had and laid it on the bed. He then called the insurance company and lawyers. "See, dad. I did what you wanted. I was the son you wanted. You can be happy with me now. I did it. See. She's dead and I have it all. All the money." But then why wasn't he happy? Why did the smile fade when he remembered her face, the horror on it? When her saw her lifeless body in the bathroom. He remembered the first time he spoke to her, the way her face lit up. He remembered the first time they had sex. He never came so hard. She was a wonderful wife. Why did he have to kill her? He lay on the bed in agony, his mind replaying moments of their life together until he eventually passed out with the money cradling his body.

Mike expected to wake up to a new day, money on the bed, but he woke up to a bed with the indentation of his wife, the covers half off, sunlight streaming in and the sounds of a shower being turned on in the master bedroom. He fell asleep in his room and woke up in hers. Mike walked down the stairs to the living room to try and think.

As before, he found himself staring into the fire. His father's shrill voice spoke to him again, urging him to kill his wife all over again. It was as if he hadn't just done it all yesterday.

"Father, I've already done this. I've already killed her, and I will not do it again. It was a mistake the first time. I can get you money some other way. I'll work overtime at the office. I'll get promoted. I can do that. I can work hard."

"Nothing you do is of any consequence. The only thing you can do is kill your wife. That's the only thing that will matter, that will help our family."

"But I've already done it!" Mike yelled.

"Well clearly you haven't done it right," his father replied angrily, as if the answer were obvious.

That had to be it. He hadn't killed her properly. That was all. Somehow, he messed up. Maybe she was alive after he went to bed? The truth was staring at him in the face, but it was too horrible for him to accept so the version his father offered seemed like a better option but in his mind, he knew the truth. He had killed her the first time.

His walked up the stairs, wanting to finally end this. He would kill his wife and be done with it. He could finally move on. He walked towards the bathroom, happily this time. He waited for just the right moment to strike. He paid no mind to her singing or her applying makeup to look good for him. None of it mattered. The only things that mattered were to be rid of a day that kept repeating and a repulsive act he didn't want to do again. This time he would make sure she was dead.

He ignored her shocked face and the twinge of pain his heart felt was less this time. The image of her lying in a pool of blood was now a relief. He checked her pulse this time to be sure. She was dead, he was free. Free from the repeating day and free from his father's tyrannical rule. Mike would gladly give his father all the money he wanted if he would just leave him alone.

Mike walked out of the bathroom into his bedroom, not sorry in the least but actually happy that he had finally done it. After years of hearing his father pound the idea into him, he finally listened. He slept on his king-size bed full of money yet again, a smile on his face.

He woke up to sunlight in his face. He would have to get better blinds. He placed his hand on the side, next to him, his eyes still closed, expecting money to be there, but there was only an indentation of his wife with the blankets half off.

And so the day repeated over and over and over again. All through the month of renovations for the new clients. The workers were unaware of the echo of death surrounding the place they were remodeling. The anguish was unknown to the people on the alternative plane.

No matter what Mike did, the result was the same. He tried to stop himself. Forced himself to sit on his hands thinking that if he didn't murder his wife, the day wouldn't repeat. She begged him some days not to kill her, even asked him why. He wanted to stop, he genuinely did but he couldn't. That's just the thing, his hands and body wouldn't let him remain idle. They had a mind of their own and even when he tried to force himself to stop, glued his hands to the chair, they always found a way to grab the poker and kill his wife. He felt possessed, not in control of his own body.

The day had repeated so many times, he felt as though he was going insane. He was laughing at the shadows on the wall and the fireplace. He tried to burn down the house, run to her and warn her but nothing worked. The same result happened every time. She died by his hand, sometimes with a different weapon, but always dead in the bathroom. He thought he was cursed. He tried to leave the house, but he couldn't. The door wouldn't open. His cellphone had no service. He thought he saw shadows moving around in his house, but he couldn't seem to find out where they were or speak to them. He was alone and terrified. All the abuse from his father paled in comparison to the horror of the situation he found himself in now.

He woke up again for what felt like the 100th time. He could hear a car driving onto the property. That was new, odd really. Was this day somehow special? Maybe this day was the day he could save her and end all of this.

He slowly walked up the stairs unsure of what to do, anxiety ever present, his stomach turning in knots. His posture was rigid, his palms sweaty. He made it to the bathroom and the weapon was in his hands. This time a knife. That was different as well. Usually he had to pick up the weapon, unwillingly of course. This time it simply appeared in his hand. *How strange.* The second, Mike got to the doorway, he could hear the song that Mary was singing. It was a love song. Every time and he had never noticed. 100 times and he had never really listened. She really loved him, trusted him even. His gut twisted with that knowledge. He really didn't want to do this. He would rather do anything but this.

He let go of the knife and it fell but froze in mid-air, not falling to the floor and the next second it was back in his hand. He tried again only to get the same result.

His feet carried him into the bathroom but this time there was a creak of the floorboards under his feet, a loud one, an unmistakable sound and Mary tensed. Or did the creaking sound come from the alternate plane, from the movers or the real estate agent. One can't be sure, but this time Mary heard the creak, this time she had a warning.

Figuring that since this day was happening differently, he thought that there might be a chance to end it one way or another. He then proceeded to drop things on the floor, so she would know. He tried to purposely make more noise. In all the previous times when the day repeated, he had never done that. He heard a car pull up to the house. Did someone call the police? Is this finally over?

"Mike? Baby, are you okay? Is that you?"

He wanted to yell, "No, it's an intruder, kill him and run," but he said nothing. He just stood there shaking. He clutched the knife, willing himself to turn around but knowing that he couldn't.

"Please, I've learned my lesson. I've repented this act. Let tomorrow happen. Please. I don't want to do this. It was wrong. I know that now. Please stop me," he begged in a whisper, to anyone listening with the power to change his fate.

"It's too late. Too late to change. You're already dead," a strange voice told him, a voice he had never heard before. A voice that sounded like it spoke through the house, a large booming voice that nearly shook the foundations.

"Don't make me do this again. I don't want to kill her. I don't want her to die. I want my life back," he pleaded with the voice. But silence was the only response he got.

He heard footsteps walking up to the house, boots grinding on the gravel and then a key being put into a lock. There were footsteps in the house, heavy ones and someone was talking. What was happening?

Mike tried to figure it out, momentarily distracted from his cause to murder. Who were these people? He tried to listen to their words and observe them. To do so, he had to move away from the bathroom and lean over the railing.

He saw a couple walking into their house? What were they doing here? This was his house! Mike leaned even farther over the railing unknowingly at the right vantage point for Mary to see a knife in the mirror. She couldn't see the rest of him, just the knife.

She gasped and furiously looked around the bathroom for a weapon. She couldn't find any. She did what she had to. She smashed the mirror. Mike whirled around at the sound as did the new clients.

They came running up the stairs. Mike turned to Mary just as she grabbed a shard of glass and stabbed him in the heart.

"Why," she asked, her face full of pain and anguish.

"For the money," Mike said sheepishly.

"I loved you with everything I had."

"I know. You always deserved better. I should never have married you. I should never have listened to my father. I should have killed him, not you. I'm so sorry, Mary. Please forgive me," he pleaded in a forlorn voice. A moment later there was a faint smile on his lips. Finally, he understood the horror of his actions and it was finally over. She had killed him. He knew instantly when he fell to the ground that the repeat was over.

The last thought Mike had was to wonder whether this is what was meant to happen all along. How fitting for *his* murder to be the one that ended the repeating day. He heard Mary screaming over his body, trying to save him but it's too late. "Thank you, Mary," were his last words to her.

The young couple ran into the bathroom not seeing Mary, but she saw them. She looked at them with wild, confused and angry eyes. She calmed when she noticed how much this woman's husband loved her, how he protectively grabbed her to prevent her from getting close to the broken mirror. He loved his wife as much as she though Mike had loved her. The woman's husband hugged her close when a chill went over her body.

The real estate agent looked around worriedly. Were the ghosts here now? Were there really ghosts in the house? "I am so sorry about all that noise. That's very strange. It's never happened before. I'll get someone in to fix the mirror right away," she assured the couple.

The couple nodded, and the second Jenny left, they kissed each other, a passionate loving kiss. They went down to open the door for the movers again. The movers had already moved some of their things inside earlier.

The couple laughed, so happy to be here, together in their new house. Their love for each other visible in every look, every touch. Mary had no choice but to enter the woman, desperate to find the love Mike had never given her -- to find a man worthy of the devotion and love she had shown Mike. Home at last!

———————————

EIGHT

A Fine Day for Murder

I walk into the small shop, to get my morning coffee as I always do, only to be met with a line. *A line*! I hate lines. If only they knew who I was, I wouldn't have to wait in a bloody line. But they don't, and it's early in the morning. Too early to make that much of a fuss. Suffer quietly it is.

I have to keep wearing this mask of normalcy at least until I reach my apartment, my safe haven for the monster I really am.

Being a normal citizen is getting increasingly harder when there are so many people -- people who are so very happy, chatting away without a care in the world. Very weird. Happy in the morning? I don't think I've ever been happy in the morning even *with* coffee. Coffee just stops my mind from thinking too much, delving into darker thoughts. Maybe true happiness isn't for people like *me* anyway. *Always with the deep thoughts before I have my coffee. I'm so goddamn melodramatic. And there I go with the inner monologue. I need some caffeine for sure, and I need to get to work.*

Someone just rushes past me to get on the line. I barely suppress a growl. What, he can't wait a few minutes and stand behind me? No, he has to run ahead. Too bad the floor isn't slippery. I would laugh if he fell and broke his head open. *Yep, right on cue with the dark thoughts. Gotta love my brain.* Aside from the rudeness and how inconsiderate his actions are, I move a bit to make sure his shoulders don't touch mine. This is a designer suit. I don't need his kind rubbing off on my fine silk suit. The cleaners can't get asshole out of a suit, so best to steer clear.

I stand there proudly, finally on the line, glowering at the people in front of me. I actually start counting. I casually look behind me and hold my head up high. So many more people are behind me, waiting on *me* to order. If they had come earlier, they would have been in my spot. *Ha.* That pride dissipates quickly, as I'm reminded that there are six people in front of me! Six! Kill me now. Hmm...speaking of killing...Oh, I've got it. What a fun game I've come up with. What a perfect way to spend the time since I already know what I'll order. Why order any other drink aside from my usual? Why pay money for a *chance* to like your drink? How idiotic. This way I *know* what I'm getting every time. I *know* I'll love it. *That's* the smart choice.

OMG! How do you honestly get to the front of the line and still have no idea what you want? What were you doing in the line? Picking your nose? Spacing out? I mean *seriously*! It's a coffee shop. What kind of coffee do you like? It's not a tough question. You like coffee with milk? Go with a latte. Apparently to him, the question of what one would want is the end all, be all of questions ever asked in the history of time! Not like I'm dying for coffee. The line behind you -- means nothing. Take your time. Now onto my game...

I imagine pouring hot steaming coffee on his face and saying, "Couldn't make a decision, eh? Well here's your coffee." I can hear his screams in my mind, see his skin bubbling and peeling as it leaves his bones. *Oh...well that was a bit much at 10 am.* My mind is now satisfied and he is now mentally taken off the line, even though in reality, he's still talking to the barista. The aim of this murderous game is to mentally kill everyone in front of me so I can get my coffee NOW and not in twenty minutes. So, one customer down, five to go.

The next in line is a Brooklyn hipster judging by the tight jeans. Do girls like that? Seeing his ass in his jeans? I suppose it's tight everywhere. Sexual politics boiled down to jeans. Wow. How to kill him? Hmm… Wait a minute. Didn't he bring a scarf? Okay, low hanging fruit I know but uh… why not use it? Bit lazy on my part but it'll do. *It's hard to come up with creative kills on no coffee. I'm trying my best, brain.* I'm usually one for theatrics but the image of mentally strangling him from behind is a fun one. He would turn around wide-eyed, asking why. I'd simply state, "I wanted my coffee now and you were talking too long. Too bad for you. How about a caramel stole latte?" Ok, it's not *technically* precise since he's wearing a scarf, not quite a stole but it'll do. I chuckle at it all the same. Not a bad line. Tad dorky but again, best I can do at 10 am. Anyway, onto the next one.

Next up is a businessman who thinks his time is precious. Join the club, bucko. So an arrogant businessman? I gotta take him down a peg. And here he goes checking his huge watch again? Time is clearly important to him. Maybe I'd smash his watch and kill him with the shards of glass. Yes, I'd kill him with what he loves most. Time itself. That has to be the most unique murder, right? Kill him with his own watch, kill him with time itself! It does have a certain flair to it after all. Imagine the shock on his face as I rush toward him shoving his wrist into the wood counter, smashing his watch. He would be hurling epithets left and right. I would smile calmly and slowly retrieve a small sliver of glass and in a few seconds, he would be dead. I'm very efficient at what I do. I would quickly slit his throat, and that would be that. Another one down.

Then there's a woman who is quite gorgeous but sad. Her eyes look weary and tired. She's wearing a faded black backpack with a school ID hanging down from one of the pockets. I never enjoy killing women, much prefer to stick to my own gender unless provoked. She could get a pass. She looks like she needs caffeine desperately. Poor girl. I would kill everyone else just to quicken it for her. See doctor I feel sympathy. I can empathize with my fellow humans. Take that Dr. Connor! I'm an empathetic serial killer.

Next, there's a woman with a child. I never kill children or mothers, so she too, gets a pass. I don't even have to think about it. It's done. She's safe. Maybe… a creepy warning with a bloody knife if she takes forever to order. I would never EVER harm mothers or children, *but* she wouldn't know that, so she'd hurry. *Problem solved.*

Next up, we got a skateboard kid. Isn't a thirty-year-old man too old for that? I think so. What? Your car broke down on your way to work and you just happened to have a skateboard in your bag? Your work is okay with you getting there on a skateboard? I'm going to rule out a lawyer then. This is lazy yet again, but come on, he brought his own murder weapon! It's almost *too* perfect. How could I not use it? I can imagine shoving him to the ground and grabbing his skateboard from his sweaty hands. A grimace would form on my face. I'd ignore his angry cries and slam the skateboard on his skull over and over again. Knowing me, I'd probably stop to take a gander at the blood splatter. I never saw blood splatter from a skateboard before. It'd be tough to clean up and I've been a killer for so many years now. It's the only thing that makes me truly happy, the only thing I'm really good at. And to go to jail and be caught after all this time because of some man with a skateboard? Oh, how ignominious! But for good coffee, I suppose it would be worth it. They can arrest me after I have my cup.

Murder and coffee have been the only two stable things in my life. I long for a good woman, a mother to my future children, but murder is hereditary or rather the propensity for this kind of murder is. My children will inherit my sickness, my darkness. Is it fair to knowingly damn a child to this life?

The question is moot anyway because no woman will ever love me for long. I can't allow it. I always keep them at a distance and when they get a whiff of darker thoughts from me, a hint of the dark mind behind my blue eyes, I drop them. I don't like causing them pain. I can feel emotions; anger is easy, happiness is harder, and love is complicated, but I can feel them. I don't like hurting them, but the alternative is murdering them. And I refuse to do that -- not to women I care about. But I can't get caught so leaving them is what I have to do.

I love it early on in a relationship, when I start to feel things long since dormant: a buzz, an excitement, a curiosity of what's to come. Something akin to happiness. My heart beats faster when I text her, when I am around her. I'm in a buzz the whole day before I meet her again, looking forward to a wonderful evening. I plan furiously to sweep her off her feet, hang on every word she says, strive to make her laugh with every breath. I live for the way they see me in the beginning. It's the real reason why I keep coming to this place. For the chance to experience all of that again. It's been too long since I last held a woman in my arms.

The barista. I don't even know her name. She never wears a name tag. I've been here for months but I never got up the courage to ask her out because the fallout is so painful. I always chicken out and think it's not worth it. I've coveted her from afar for way too long. I love the coffee from this place, but when it ends, and it will eventually, I'll have to find other coffee, but for now, I can have her *and* the coffee.

She looks like an angel smiling at each customer in turn, no matter what they say to her. She has soft, kind eyes that look like they could understand the psychosis, the evil inside me. She has a petite figure that would fit so well inside my strong arms. I'd promise to keep her safe and safe she would be. There is no safer than in the arms of a monster. I will literally stop at nothing to keep her safe and happy. I would do anything. What so-called good guy would literally do anything? Yeah, thought so. She's safer with me. Today is when I will ask her out. Strange though, that her coworker isn't here. That explains how slow everything is. Poor girl has to do twice the work for half the pay.

Maybe her coworker called in sick? Whatever the case, I'm finally next. My hands are sweaty, and I wipe them against my suit, cringing at the fact that I just messed it up. I will now have to clean it, yet again. I waited while the man in front of me, "Mr. Skateboard," tried to talk to her. To MY barista. I suppress every urge in my body to bash his head in right then and there and throw her over my shoulder like a caveman. I sigh at my own impulses, but they quickly return. How dare he talk to MY barista! As if I had any right to be possessive over a woman who I can't seem to gather up the nerve to talk to. She smiles courteously at him but isn't giving any sign that she actually enjoys "Mr. Skateboard" being in her space. The smile seems to be one of forced politeness and not at all genuine. In fact, she looks my way and smiles a real genuine smile. A smile just for me. But that dear reader, isn't what surprised me. No, it was the blood on her sleeve, the slightest bit of blood. Anyone else would have missed it, but not me. Blood on her sleeve...missing coworker...hmm. How curious. Could it be? Probably not. I've never been that lucky so far. She probably had a nose bleed or cut herself shaving or -- I don't know -- got a paper cut even. Who cares? She's not a murderer! I mean look at her. She can't possibly be like me and eventually I'll have to break her heart like all the rest. I should enjoy this while it lasts. Wow, talk about somber, I really need coffee.

I finally make it to the front. I feel like I ran a marathon or discovered the cure for cancer. It seems like a huge feat and now of course, I forgot my order. *How hilarious.* Too many thoughts are in my head at once. Now I'm at the front looking at the menu, undoubtedly holding up the line.

The barista smiles warmly at me as she leans in, smelling of delicious rich black coffee. "Hi. I see you in here a lot."

All suave mannerisms lost as I stumble over my words. *Great first impression.* "I--I uh forgot."

She laughs a soft laugh before placing a hand quickly over mine. "Happens to all of us. Don't worry, I know your usual order." Her voice is so intoxicating, chipper but not high pitched, lower than most women, a voice from a *film noir.* I have no idea why I never noticed it before. It's so enthralling.

"Your coworker isn't here," I state pointedly, kicking myself for not flirting. *Could it have killed me to flirt? Don't I know how to flirt? When did I forget how to talk to a girl?*

I watch her tense up minutely and then plaster a fake smile onto her face. "Nope. Flying solo today..."

I smirk at that. So she's a beginning murderer then. Well, she could use an old, experienced murderer to show her the way. Help her avoid the many pitfalls, show her how to clean up crime scenes, etc. I would of course be happy to offer my services. How magnanimous of me, giving back to my community and all.

"Connor," I say confidently reaching out to shake her hand.

"Becca, nice to meet you," she replies, eyeing me carefully, trying to assess if I'm a friend or foe.

"Charmed to meet you." I hold her hand and turn her arm around slowly, to draw attention to the blood splatter on her sleeve. I look down at it pointedly, to further draw her attention there. "Don't be frightened, kitten, you're not the only murderer here," I whisper to her. I wasn't even sure she heard until I saw her freeze and a slow sly smile that I never saw before creeps onto her face, a smile that transforms her once soft and sweet face into one of a sly temptress.

"You're very observant," Becca states, her eyes sparkling with mischief.

"Murderers usually are," I reply with a chuckle.

Becca rings up my order in silence after eyeing the long crowd behind me. I hand her exact change and scribble my number on the back of a five-dollar bill. I did the deed; gave Becca my number, flirted, told her we were the same, game over for now. There was no need to hold up the line any longer, but the words won't come out. She is the one woman who makes me nervous, powerless against her strong, feminine aura.

Becca smirks and hides the five under the register. We don't say anything else. What else could be said in public?

For the first time, I feel hope. Hope that maybe this angel was as damaged as I was. Maybe she was made for me. I walk over to a separate area to collect my coffee, feeling a pleasant buzz coursing through my whole body. I'm floating along, a king among men or so it feels.

Becca calls out my name, our fingers touch and there's a delicious spark there, so much chemistry. Her eyes sparkle as she hands me the cup. She smiles at me with that same bewitching, dark smile before returning to the counter, and pretending to be the prim and proper coffee girl everyone came in to see.

I watch her work, studying her facade, her public mask, it was incredible. She was quite the con artist. Becca smiles and laughs with the patron behind me. I stood there mesmerized and a bit confused. Had I truly seen a darker side to Becca or did I just imagine it? My longings creating an illusion to quell my desire? That's when I looked down at the to-go cup, she had written on it.

"Finally, a man who enjoys a little murder now and again. My coworker, Amanda was such an annoying and judgmental person. I just couldn't take her level of negativity, day after day. Don't you just hate people like that? I'll probably have to leave this town soon. Call me and we can leave together. Tonight, would be best. My number is on the back.

XOXO- Becca

I wasn't imagining anything. Becca *was* like me, with the same disease. If I had a soul, I'd say we were soulmates, but people like us don't have souls. Looking at what she wrote brought me so much joy. Leave together? Like a dream come true. Who knew I'd find my other half in a coffee shop?

———————————

NINE

Desire

Desire. What an ostentatious name for a club but it sufficed. It was the living embodiment of sin itself. Anything you desired could be found here, all for the cheap price of your soul or a few measly dollars. With an "Open Nightly" sign on the outside door, it was a place where the hopeless could come to find solace, a haven for lost souls. It was for those men or women who weren't much more than blank slates waiting to be filled with emotions. It was a place where the broken became whole and where you found exactly what you needed -- if you were desperate enough.

Alana was a dancer, but she didn't dance for money or for the affections of the idiotic, pitiful excuses for humans that frequented this place. No, she danced for the chance to make the acquaintance of a powerful vampire. In a place like this she had hoped to find one by now but all she had found thus far were other equally lost souls. That is, until tonight, when her life would change in more ways than she could ever fathom.

Once, many moons ago, she had worked as an assassin killing monsters who preyed on innocents. In the beginning she was moralistic, righting wrongs. *Yes, how arrogant. I know.* And then, she began to crave the violence and the adrenaline, the rush she got from a good fight. The violence became an outlet for her rage and pain.

She grew up alone, fighting the good fight but never getting close to others. She preferred to isolate herself from the world. These days, you never know who people really are. Your neighbors, your best friend could secretly be a monster underneath. It's not like villains had tell-tale signs; this wasn't a movie. Monsters existed, and they could look like anyone. So part of her isolation was to avoid getting close to someone she'd eventually have to kill. Make no friends, befriend no monsters – her unofficial slogans. But her isolation from mankind was more than that. She was guarding herself against getting hurt, against letting the wrong people in so she never let anyone in.

When Alana got the itch, she found someone to scratch it. No names, no commitments, no strings, just a pleasurable night and nothing more. It made her feel less angry about the sudden death of her parents. People said monsters killed them, but Alana never knew for certain. The anger at suddenly being thrust into a world she wanted no part of, with monsters around every corner, monsters that killed her parents, lessened over time. But when children are exposed to this at such an early age, it affects them, taints their worldview. And the Agency filled that fear and uncertainty of being in a scary world with the dark purpose of killing monsters.

Over time there grew a blank space in her soul that never got filled with kindness or love. It just remained empty. Alana never had much in the way of family after her parents' death. Her foster family was nothing to brag about. She never had a model for a happy successful relationship or for the love she secretly desired but found frightening and distasteful. Alana thought love was an illusion, the punch-line on a greeting card and nothing more.

She grew colder, more isolated, and then on a job she slipped up. It was a messy kill. There was a large group of vampires instead of just a couple. Talk about bad intel. She barely got out alive and accidentally got vampire blood all over herself. Some went into her mouth and it was like everything suddenly made sense. That drop of blood changed everything.

Alana felt connected to the universe, more confident, powerful beyond human comprehension. Sounds and tastes were more intense. Vampire blood became a drug she couldn't quit. Nothing had ever made her that happy. The blood spoke to her, called to her like a dark lullaby. It took only a short amount of time until the bloodlust became a serious addiction that defined her whole life.

The withdrawal symptoms were not something she could live with. Alana's heart raced, she felt weak, and vomited for days without it. Withdrawal was horrible and painful. Blood was calling to her, she was a slave to it. Thoughts of blood haunted every facet of her waking life. And her dreams were filled with murder. It wasn't like there were meetings or recovery programs for blood addicts. There was only one remedy for this, drinking vampire blood. The Agency didn't offer her any jobs for a week and a half. So, there was no outlet for her addiction, no chance to distract herself with murdering monsters. No hope of finding vampires. Alana was slowly dying without it.

When the Agency did finally call her in for a job, the elders promptly found out about her little addiction. They saw how she reacted to vampire blood and that was the end of her illustrious career. They said she was a monster herself. *Please, how dramatic.*

They left her with only two options; find a vampire or die. The old men, the Elders in the Agency, the ones who hired young women and children to kill monsters, wanted her to die like a junkie in an alleyway but tonight she would find a vampire, she had to. She wasn't dying because old men decided it. They made her a junkie and she was going to be an awesome one at that. Maybe she'd even find love. Maybe she'd find a way to dismantle the Agency and free everyone from a life like hers: isolated, damaged, and alone.

The music swelled; she'd have to go out there soon. Alana's heart was beating out of her chest and her hands were shaking with need. The world was beginning to look dismal again and she felt a wave of depression come over her at the banality of life itself. But none of that mattered, she had to ensnare a vampire; there was no other option.

Alana kept her head steady and smiled almost genuinely. She

waved to her adoring fans and put on a good show. She closed her eyes and pretended that the accolades and claps were enough to keep her going but that's never what she'd been after. All the same, it felt nice to be in a room full of people who enjoyed her presence.

Kieran was never one for clubs in general but this one always drew him in. He rather liked the blatant disregard for what was proper. Sins were displayed, deals made, blood flowed, entertainment sought out, all in the open, mind you. No back-alley dealings. It was liberating and quite literally the devil's playground. He came here to be among like-minded people, which he needed. He was ridiculed by his brother, Tristan for his addiction, even called "weak," because of it. His brother knew nothing of what Kieran was going through. On paper maybe, it *was* ridiculous. A vampire addicted to human blood? But so what? He was still the leader of the most ruthless clan of vampires and that should have afforded him at least a modicum of respect. Not ridicule from his own brother, whose laughter in the matter was quite distasteful.

Kieran literally ran out in search of this club because he knew his time was up. His brother wouldn't be able to keep his addiction quiet. Tristan wanted Kieran's throne and telling the others of his brother's addiction would be the perfect way to unseat him. This club was Kieran's last hope, his only hope to survive the coming decades. He had to find a willing human who wouldn't be repelled by his addiction but instead would happily supply him with what he needed. He in turn would treasure her and make her his Queen. Would there be anyone worthy of either? Only time would tell. If he was being truly honest with himself, he was also looking for love. He would never tell anyone this, but centuries of loneliness weighed on him.

If he didn't find a human and couldn't give up his addiction, he might very well be killed by his own people in an uprising. Hell, he wouldn't blame them. Who wants a vampire leader with a human blood addiction? His head was on the chopping block; he could feel it.

Kieran downed his whiskey as he glanced around rather apathetically. No one ever caught his attention, but he couldn't leave, not yet. Not until he found a human or got up the courage to face his fate with his own kind. More whiskey was in order. He signaled the bartender.

Kieran sighed heavily. Everyone was too pedestrian for his liking. All the same his eyes followed Alana as she walked onto the stage. He squinted his eyes feeling an undeniable pull to this woman. *How have I missed this ravishing creature? Is she new? I should have come to this place sooner,* he mused.

For some inexplicable reason Kieran couldn't look away. His eyes ran up and down Alana's figure already entranced by her. Her face brought back memories of a woman he loved a long time ago, before he was a vampire.

Alana's dress swayed with her as she glided across the stage dancing seductively, not for the men cheering, but for herself. She loved dancing. She never felt freer than when she danced. Alana became one with the song, getting lost in the words, letting them glide over her skin like a gentle caress. She moved her body sensually, arching her back and gliding her hand over her figure. Alana's hips swayed in time to the beat as her hands moved up her body and past her neck to tousle her long curly red hair.

Kieran was captivated by the way she moved. *She dances like a goddess and looks like an angel. I have no idea why she works in a place like this but surely, she isn't looking for me, is she? Could an angel like that really be hiding something dark and damaged? Luck's never been on my side before, why count on it now? If she were looking for me or my kind, I would treasure her. I wonder if her blood would taste as sweet as she looks. She is at least a welcome distraction from my brother. I'll give her that.*

All the other dancers Kieran saw usually took their clothes off to hoots and hollers from the crowd, the very basest of dancing. But Alana, no. She was a shining example of sensual dancing and how affecting one can be even *with* clothes on.

Alana's eyes were closed almost the entire time. She much preferred to dance unhindered by the audience. She wasn't too keen on seeing some random stranger's lustful gaze. She wasn't for sale and she wasn't looking to tease or tempt anyone. This way she didn't give any man the wrong idea. She was dancing for herself; the men just happened to be there.

Towards the end of the song, though, Alana felt a strong presence staring at her, boring a hole in the back of her head. It was intense, and it felt like a rope being tugged. She opened her eyes almost too abruptly and locked eyes with an attractive, intense older man dressed impeccably. *Wow, that's who's been looking at me? Oh, honey, you don't have to stop on my account. Tall, dark and definitely dangerous? Just my type. Now if he's a vampire, I just hit the jackpot. He's drinking whiskey, and he looks like he knows how to seduce -- not that he has to try that hard. Any woman here would want him but he's looking at me. Drinking in my dance, my body. Better give him a real good show. Show him what I can do and if he's a good boy, what I can do for him later.*

He drank his whiskey slowly, savoring the taste on his tongue, swirling it around. His eyes never left hers. The stranger's tailored silk shirt was tight around his muscular arms and his pants seemed to be quite tight as well. He was appraising her and demanding she come to him all at once. The strange pull she felt only got stronger.

The rest of the set is for you, big boy. Enjoy. Her dance changed from one of self-expression to one of seduction

The lights on the stage turned red, bathing her in a rather ominous glow. She couldn't be sure, but she could have sworn his eyes turned pitch black and looked hungrier and more intense. *Dangerous indeed and possibly not human.*

Alana made sure to arch her back more and to show off all of her assets. Judging by the heated look he was giving her and the fact that he was white knuckling the table, she was quite sure he got the message.

Her set was over a minute later. Alana walked down from the stage gracefully only to flag down a server. Kieran's heart raced as she walked. Was it to speak to him? That's the custom here. Ladies choice always. Introductions had to be made by a server to initiate any conversation or make contact with someone you didn't come in with. Anyone who didn't abide by the rules was promptly kicked out. Kieran saw Alana look over at him. He wished he could hear the conversation but even with his super hearing, the club was too loud to eavesdrop. There was too much ambient noise, two songs playing at the same time amid a flurry of loud conversations.

"Who is that man over there, who's making his affections quite clear?" Alana asked the server, biting her lip in anticipation.

The server offered no explanation, diving right into a practiced question with an equally practiced smile. "Do you share those affections ma'am?"

A slow smile crept onto her face, "I very much do."

Finally, after a moment, but to Kieran it seemed like several minutes, the server walked towards him. When he reached Kieran, the server smiled and held out his hand. Kieran nodded and held his glass up to Alana, the universal sign. The server then waved her over to Kieran's table.

"Mr. Kieran, this is the lovely Alana. If you should need anything further, don't hesitate to contact me. My name is Pete. Thank you for choosing Desire to meet your needs."

"Quite chatty, isn't he," Kieran said, the second the man left.

"They're big on rules here. He was only going by the guidebook," Alana offered.

Kieran grinned at Alana as she slowly sat down beside him. "Ah, but life is more interesting when you bend the rules, isn't it pet?"

"Indeed, it is," she said with a genuine smile, feeling happy conversing with him, a happiness she hadn't felt in years. *Smooth and sexy*, she thought. She felt an even stronger pull now that they were this close. Alana couldn't help her eyes as they drifted down his shirt to his pants, his tight, constrained pants. She licked her lips unconsciously. Out of the corner of her eye, Alana saw a bartender flit by. She really needed a drink. With a flick of her hair and a dainty little twist of her wrist, the bartender came over.

With a smile Alana said, "I'll have what he's having."

"Adventurous, are we?" Kieran teased.

"Nothing beats an aged whiskey, old, full-bodied, delicate yet fiery and all the while comforting," Alana said truthfully meaning both the whiskey and the mysterious Kieran.

"What an eloquent way to describe whiskey. I'll have another as well."

"Isn't it just," Alana replied with a smirk. The bartender came back quickly with the whiskeys. *So, he's someone important. He served us immediately over all her other orders. Hmm.* She was even more intrigued about Kieran and hoped he would be more forthcoming as the night wore on.

Alana smiled as she ran her fingers along the edge of her glass. "So, what is that you do, Kieran?"

The man beside her visibly tensed before answering. He pretended to be undeterred by the question even going so far as to scoff as if he were offended. "No, no banal questions. That's beneath you, darling. Besides I rather like the game we're playing, and I don't want to lose when I've just started."

Alana raised her eyebrow. "I don't frighten easy. I work here after all."

"Bit unusual for a girl such as yourself to work here of all places, no?" Kieran inquired, actually curious to see what she'd say.

Alana slipped her hand into his open one and watched as he slowly took her hand and brought it to his lips for a kiss.

"Ever the gentleman, good to know. Maybe I belong here. Maybe I have a darker side. Wouldn't you love to find out?"

"I very much would," Kieran admitted with a slight growl.

"Someone's getting all hot and bothered. Now, now, down boy. A handsome devilish man such as yourself looks a tad out of place here. You're wearing a thousand-dollar suit and let's not even mention the handmade leather shoes you're wearing. Everyone else is less refined, more outwardly evil, or rather looks like a cartoon villain, even in a gorgeously decorated den of iniquity as this is. So, what brings you here, might I ask?

"Looks can be deceiving."

"How interesting. Are you a villain? I happen to have a small space in my heart for villains. I assure you when it comes to myself, looks can be deceiving as well. I'm no damsel."

"Duly noted," he replied as he raised his glass to toast with Alana. He waited until she lifted her glass up as well and then he downed the burning liquid. He licked his lips and then seemed as if he were lost in thought. Alana simply watched him, growing rather curious about the sophisticated and decidedly evil man next to her. When he didn't say anything, she spoke up, twisting around in the booth to look at him straight on.

"I've been wondering about something all night, and while I love our witty repartee, it's been gnawing at me. May I ask you a bold question?"

Kieran raised her eyebrows urging her to go on. "I dare say you've intrigued me. Go ahead, darling."

Alana moved in closer to really study him. She was sure she already knew the answer, but she wanted his verbal affirmation. She could smell blood on him, and curiously leather and a deliciously woodsy smell not to mention the whiskey on his breath. She carefully moved closer to him, so she could study his eyes. You can lie with words but very few people can lie with their eyes. Alana was close enough now that he could feel the warmth of her breath on his neck. He remained stock still, his arms on the back of the booth lest he make a wrong move. His hands were itching to touch her, grab her onto his lap and drink her blood. Feast on her but not kill her. No, she was far too intriguing for that.

Alana whispered seductively in his ear, "Are you by any chance a vampire?"

He froze in place at that question. Alana saw fear, surprise and awe pass over his face before a smirk settled on it. *Does his silence mean I'm wrong? If so, I have to find a vampire and no matter how alluring, this man is I have to get up right now. Honestly, I'm not sure I could do that. I really like this guy. Wait a minute, was he amused by my question? If so why stay silent? What's the end game here? How frustrating. Come on, hot stuff, give a girl something to go on!*

Kieran saw panic flit across Alana's face and he furrowed his eyebrows. *How very curious. Maybe she is darker than I gave her credit for. Afraid that I'm not a vampire? This little slip of thing is looking for my kind? Wants to give herself to my kind? I won't have it. She's all mine. I'll take good care of her, not like some vampires I know. I couldn't see this dynamic little spitfire as simply food. No, she's so much more. It's my lucky day after all.*

Alana's tone lost all feistiness and became needy, desperate even. "Please. I-I'm looking for a vampire." She placed her hand on his elbow which made him look at her more closely. He was rather happy with her desperate need for a vampire, but he needed to know why first.

His voice took on the tone of a father chastising his daughter, "Silly girl why would you be looking for a vampire? You know what...."

Alana cut Kieran off before he could even finish his sentence, growing more desperate by the minute. "I'm addicted to vampire blood," she confessed as she ran her hand over his suit feeling the contours of his lapel. She needed to know if he was a vampire. She had given so much away but she was so desperate, and she felt so connected to him. She couldn't stop touching him. His suit felt so soft under her fingers.

Without any further hesitation, Kieran pulled her into this chest, his arms loosely wrapped around her lower back. Alana smiled up at him, welcoming the embrace. Kieran breathed in her scent; the strong, vanilla, amber and flower scent of her perfume and the sweet lingering smell of her honeysuckle and lavender shampoo.

His voice was soft and gentle, gone was any teasing or harsh tone. He spoke quietly so that only Alana could hear his confession. "I am indeed a vampire, my dear, who just happens to be addicted to human blood." Alana was so relieved and happy to have found such a perfect connection that she actually laughed. They were addicted to each other's blood. It's as if fate had brought them to the club tonight. Kieran smiled as he watched Alana. He liked seeing her happy and her smile lit up the room. He felt so connected to her, so focused on her that everyone else ceased to exist.

"You know, I've been coming here for a while now and I never found any vampires much less vampires that would be okay with my addiction. I never knew vampires could be addicted to human blood. I would think you'd see us as food and that's it."

He tensed at her words fearing a judgmental response coming next, fearing that this beautiful creature would call him, "weak," like Tristan, but she never did. The criticism never came.

Alana noticed his body language and shook her head. Her hand came up to caress his cheek tenderly. "No judgment here. We're both addicts here for a fix and I'd be happy to help you if you return the favor."

Kieran nodded though he honestly wasn't sure he could just do that. He was so taken by her that the thought of drinking from her and leaving her moments later, left him feeling angry and bereft at the same time. What a strange feeling for one who has been alone for centuries.

Alana kept her touches gentle so as not to spook him. Kieran smiled down at her and they knew then and there that this would probably go beyond just blood.

"Let's get a booth in the back," Alana suggested. "Behind the goons and the curtain."

Kieran chuckled at her choice of words. "Someone so delicate and good yet so broken. What happened, my darling, to make you like this?"

"I could ask you the same thing."

Kieran chuckled. "I'm dangerous, pet. This is a dangerous game you can't hope to win," he warned her.

Alana smiled a wistful smile. "I'm not looking to win. I just need to feel alive."

"I'm not just any vampire. I'm the leader of the Cavanaughs."

Everyone heard whispers of them. They ruled this small town. They were ruthless and evil or so the rumors went. Alana could see the weariness and the danger in his eyes but the way he talked, the way he held her was anything but dangerous.

A soft smile appeared on Alana's face as she looked at Kieran, "Well, aren't I a lucky girl? You look so weary and tired. Just come with me, Kieran and I'll take care of you. I mean you no harm. Let's feed our addictions safely. We need each other. We were made for each other. Two parts of a puzzle."

He touched her cheek softly and studied her eyes to see if she was telling the truth. Kieran slowly snapped his fingers and teleported Alana and himself to an unoccupied velvet-covered booth at the back of the club. The bouncers, being vampires, knew they were there but had the good sense not to comment. The black curtain hid them from the rest of the club. No one even looked their way.

Privacy was key in this place, the most important rule, and especially so when Kieran Cavanaugh came around.

Alana and Kieran sat down, sitting as close to each other as possible. "Are you absolutely sure, Alana?" Kieran inquired, needing her verbal confirmation, so he called her by name and not as he already had a habit of doing, by a term of endearment.

"I'm sure, Kieran," she answered confidently.

With a flourish of his wrist and a rather loud snap, Kieran made two syringes appear in either hand.

In a matter of minutes, both of them were shooting blood through their veins, a blissed out look on their faces. Kieran closed his eyes feeling a flurry of competing emotions wash over him. The emotions were so rich and intense they awakened dormant parts of his psyche. Alana in turn felt like she was floating above everything. The world around her disappeared. The club became blurry, so she closed her eyes feeling a euphoria settle over her entire being. She felt invincible and truly happy.

Somewhere in the club there was a commotion, yelling, screaming, people running, chairs flying, but Alana paid it no mind lost to the feelings. Kieran ignored it as well until he heard his name. Fear ripped him out of the happy haze of emotions as he grabbed Alana and carried her in his arms running towards the exit. A server stationed by the door sprang into action and held it open for Kieran.

Shots rang out and a knife was thrown in their direction. If it hadn't been for the server, one of them would have been dead. The server had stepped in front of Kieran and took the hit himself. Alana stared back in confusion wondering what the swirling dots were and why there was so much red on the floor.

Kieran ran with her in his arms. Alana looked behind her and saw several angry men with intense black eyes staring at her. She was still under the effects of the blood, so their eyes looked disembodied almost and so much creepier. She shivered, and Kieran simply held her tightly. He snapped his fingers and teleported before the vampires could catch up to them. Alana heard Kieran whisper an apology to her, but the words sounded foreign in her still blissed out mind.

Kieran placed Alana into a seat by the pharmacy section in a discount store, one of the few "five and dimes" still in business in a quaint town far away from the debauchery they had just left. His arms were full of things he snapped into a cart. Alana almost laughed at the banality of it all.

Kieran was the first to speak. He was worried about the men that had tried to kill her. He had a feeling it might be his brother realizing that he now had a chance to rule. Either that or the Elliots, the rival clan that wanted their town. Either way it didn't bode well. But he wasn't giving Alana up. No matter what, she was his now.

His face changed when he heard her laughter. She could wipe away any dark thoughts he had with such a laugh. *Such a powerful little human she is, and all mine.* "I can see why you're addicted. Where did you go, little one?"

"Everywhere and nowhere," was Alana's rather cryptic response. He squinted his eyes at her and she simply giggled in response. "You know, I think I like you. Can you like someone at first sight?"

Kieran smiled. *She's absolutely adorable.* "I think I like you, too." He pulled her up from the chair and walked her to the checkout line. Alana sighed as she put her head on his shoulder. *Who knew I'd get to snag him. Mr. Tall, Dark and Handsome vampire who needs me just as much as I need him. I knew that club was a good idea. That was the best "trip" I've gone on. His blood is like the gold standard. I can't wait to get to know him.*

Alana looked down just now noticing that he had items in his cart. "What's all that, handsome?" she asked curiously.

"Food, darling. You have to eat and hydrate. Not letting anything happen to you. You are more precious than you know." Alana gave him a quizzical look. He has no idea why, but the words came tumbling out. "You look like a woman I knew a long time ago. I felt a connection to you instantly. You drew me to you even before your bewitching dance. Unlike everyone else in my world, you see me as someone you could like. You're the light at the end of my tunnel. I may be a monster but, in your eyes, I can be more."

Alana smiled, the blood high slowly wearing off. "That was beautiful," she replied sincerely.

Alana had only known Kieran for a short time, but he was excitement, he was a future with the promise of adventure. He would fill up the blank slate that was her soul with love, the love she never thought she'd experience. Alana smiled at Kieran as he stepped up to the counter to pay. They were both ready to start a new life together though they had no idea what that would entail or even if Kieran wanted to go back to lead his people. All he knew was that home was wherever Alana was.

———————————————

TEN

James

___

"It's freezing in here! If it were any colder, I'd think I was in the Arctic. Who turned off the heat? Hello? Is anyone listening to me? Mr. Finlay, *please* turn up the heat. It's an icebox in here," I yelled through the wall and as per usual, the Super chose to ignore me. I added a few loud bangs and reiterated my statement a couple of times for emphasis – no harm in making sure my grievance was known, but I knew it wouldn't get me anywhere. It never did. The Super in my building hardly ever worked, god forbid he'd actually do his job. He was hardly ever in his office. Rumor among the tenants has him with his mistress somewhere downtown.

Sighing I got all my warm clothes together, three sweaters, two coats, and a blanket to be exact, and slowly descended into a dreamless sleep.

The next morning, I awoke to a beautiful day. Sunlight was streaming in through my huge bay windows and birds perched on my windowsill were singing to each other. It was one of those days when you can't help but be happy. The cold spell had broken and now it was a sauna. *Of course. How typical.* I sunk into the comfy pillows, feeling like clouds were caressing me. I really loved that bed. There's nothing else like it. Yawning and stretching like a cat, I got

ready for the day. I slowly extricated myself from the bed and began
walking to the kitchen to make myself a delicious cup of black
coffee. The second the dark brew was in my hands, I smiled,
inhaling the rich scent of fresh coffee. I meandered to the door to
retrieve my morning newspaper when I found a curious little note
coupled with gorgeous flowers. There was a bouquet of lilies, roses
and dahlias, which are actually my favorite flowers, laying carefully
on my brown, rather banal welcome mat. I looked around the hallway, but it seemed my mystery man was nowhere to be seen. I
grabbed the small note written on what felt like linen paper.
Whoever left these was someone really classy, that was for sure. The
note read:

> *Hi! I'm new her*
> *Maybe you could show me the ropes some time?*
> *Hope you enjoy the flowers.*
> *Come say hi anytime.*
> *Your new neighbor,*
> *-James Apt 5E*

I jumped into the shower squealing with delight. I had a new
neighbor who fancied me enough to get me flowers. I put on tight
skinny jeans and a comfy top, playing it casual but giving him a
glimpse. Boy, did I hope he was hot and not some old guy. That
would be awkward. I hurried up the stairs to the 5th floor to thank
him. I mean, why not be neighborly? He went out of his way to get
me such a beautiful bouquet of flowers. He obviously liked me, and
he did guess right with the flowers. Least I could do is say hi. I
wonder how he knew what I liked? Did I see him in the elevator
once and we talked? I don't remember seeing any new neighbors.
The other rather chatty, gossipy tenants didn't say anything. Maybe
it was a fast move-in?

I hoped I wouldn't embarrass myself. When I've had my coffee, I
can be quite loquacious, and I might start rambling. I hoped if I did,
I'd at least ramble about something interesting. I nervously walked
up to his door, making sure to wipe my feet three times on his

welcome mat before I rang his bell, exactly three times. Some people would say I have OCD, but I don't. I just like the number three.

The second the door opened, I smiled at the handsome man in front of me. *Wow, that's my neighbor and he likes me? Today is totally my day.* My smile must have been huge, like a hanger was in it or something. He gave me a warm smile that made me relax a little bit. But not enough to really get me to loosen up. I totally froze in front of his door. How embarrassing. I was like a deer in the headlights, which made him chuckle. It was such a rich chuckle and his voice was deep and sensual. This man was pure sex and he knew it. He flashed me a confident smile before offering me his hand. I couldn't believe that a guy that like would be into me.

"I'm James."

Now it was my turn to chuckle. "I know."

"No need to be nervous, little lady. I'm a nice guy just being gentlemanly to a pretty girl who just happens to live near me."

"Lucky me."

Ah, there was that chuckle again. I would give anything to continue to be the source of that chuckle. I bit my lip trying to make this less awkward. *Think. Say something. Stop staring at his muscular chest. Stop objectifying him! Stare at his eyes. Mmm…those deep ocean blue eyes. A girl could get lost in those. Shit. Not helping. Stop drooling!* "Uhh…Hi." *Idiot. You just did that bit.* "I-I'm Laura, Laura Smith. Your neighbor. Loved the flowers by the way. How'd you know they were favorite?" I said so fast it was a wonder he understood me.

The man had the patience of a saint waiting for me to get the words out and then offering me the sweetest smile to keep me comfortable when I did.

"Hi, Laura, nice to meet you," he replied happily. " Would you like to come in?"

"You just moved in, right?"

"Yeah, still fixing things up. Don't mind the mess."

"You sure it's okay to come in?"

"Darlin' I offered. Way I see it, be rude not to."

"Well then, I'd be glad to take a look around. Mama always told me don't be rude."

He took my hand and gently led me in. He was a real gentleman and his hand fit so perfectly in mine. It was warm and a little callused as hands can get from blue collar work. *Bet he's real handy in all sorts of ways.*

His door closed gently. That was rather odd. Did he change the doors? Don't all the doors close the same in this apartment complex? Curious thing to think about really. Mine sounds like an ominous horror movie boom when closing.

"When did you move in?"

"Been here for a couple days now. Been back and forth moving things. You know how it is."

"Yeah. Right. Well, welcome. This is a great complex, people are super nice."

"I see that. I'm nice, too."

I instantly stopped speaking and looked at the ground blushing.

"You sure do look pretty blushing darlin'."

"Um…thanks…uh…yeah as I was saying um… A rundown of the apartment complex, right? The super is a bit sluggish when it comes to fixing things but that's most apartment houses. Forgive me if I'm being too forward. Uhh…probably am…but I'd love to show you around the neighborhood. There's a great Thai place a couple of blocks from here."

"Love me some Thai, Laura. Sounds great."

James went to get his leather jacket. *Heavens to Betsy, he's a bad boy too? I bet he rides a motorcycle too. Oh man, am I one lucky girl!* He was so my type and very kind. I wondered if he wasn't already married. That would be my luck.

James was the strong silent type which was great because I love to talk about everything. He was such a great listener. And an even better advice giver.

We spent the whole day together and as promised I was his town tour guide. I showed him around the neighborhood, telling him about the people I knew; the juicy gossip, the history of the town, the stores, the laundry and the library. It was so much fun I hardly saw the time pass.

I'm sure you're asking yourself why I implicitly trusted a complete stranger and gave him so much information about myself. Definitely, not the smart girl thing to do, I know. Well, if it means anything, in retrospect I wish I hadn't. I wish I had just left it as a sweet note with nice flowers and got on with my life. James in 5E would be my ruination one way or another.

He walked me to my apartment and kissed the back of my hand like a gentleman in an old movie. He tipped his hat and wished me a good night. It was all oddly sweet if not a little peculiar. It was also odd that we never met any of my other neighbors the entire day. Usually Amanda in 2E walks her dogs in the afternoon and Victor in 6E always gets lunch and coffee to write his screenplay. It was all a bit odd. And when I called my good friend Sally in 4E and told her about James, she said no one had moved into that apartment. Clearly, she didn't have her facts straight.

As the temperature dropped to freezing again at night, a strange thing happened. While I was online, I saw a news report. I kind of glazed over the title, "Violent something," focusing instead on the picture, on James's picture. I almost died right there. I knew he was too perfect to be true. He was everything I wanted in a man. Everything I dreamed about and like always the wrong person to be with. Then I read the small article. It said he had killed a woman out of jealousy in another state. I couldn't believe it. My James killed someone? Impossible. He seemed so calm and kind. I just couldn't see him going into a jealous rage and killing anyone. That was ridiculous. Maybe he had a twin or a double or was framed. He couldn't possibly be the man they thought he was.

I suddenly heard a loud knock at my door. Which was odd given how late it was. I ran to the peephole, and saw it was James. Why would he be outside my door at this hour? I didn't even hear his footsteps walking up to my door. Was he a ninja?

The news article suddenly came to mind and I became tense, confused about what to do, torn between curiously and logic. He knew I was home, so I couldn't pretend otherwise. I had stupidly given him my work schedule and anyway, the light was on. Surely, he could see the light from under the door. So much for being stealthy.

I took a deep breath. I was conflicted to say the least. The side of him that he showed me was so gentle but maybe beneath it all *did* lie a killer. I couldn't be sure. I stepped up to the door and made an excuse for not letting him in. I mean hey, I had just seen the guy like what six hours ago? *Give a girl some space, dude.* And why had he shown up right as I read the article? *How creepy.* "Hey James...I... uh... don't really...uh...feel all that good. I'm sorry. Was throwing up not twenty minutes ago." I know my voice was wavering and shaky and betrayed my fear of him. But I couldn't worry about that. My goal at the time was not letting him in, never mind lying well.

There was silence on the other side of the door, an ominous foreboding kind of silence. His voice changed from the tone it usually held to one of danger. "Shouldn't believe everything you read. Not the first to see me in a different light. Was hoping you'd be the one to give me a chance."

My brows furrowed. *What the hell was he talking about. Was he spying on me? How did he know I read the article? Was what he said a confession?* Now I knew, as a fact, that his timing wasn't coincidental. Wait, he was hoping I'd be the one to give him a chance? Implying the other girls didn't? Boy, was I in trouble.

I must have stared at the solid oak door for several minutes trying to gather my thoughts. What he said was definitely not what I imagined he would say. I was so utterly confused. I didn't know what to believe. My cozy little apartment felt stifling and the thought of James that once brought a smile to my face, now gave me the chills. The room felt cold again or was it because my fear was making me cold? We shape our own reality to some extent with our perception of things, so either could be true.

As I sat by my desk, I noticed a red dot traveling around the room. I gasped. I've seen enough crime dramas to know that some-where out in the darkness, a high-powered rifle was responsible for that red dot. I jumped under the table just as the chair splintered into a hundred pieces. *Who was shooting at me? Could it be James? How did he get to the location so fast? Wasn't he still behind the door?*

I ran into the kitchen and pushed the refrigerator to the floor without disconnecting it and crouched behind it. That way the shooter couldn't detect my body heat. Thank god for movies and TV shows.

I heard silence, deafening silence. And then multiple voices in the hallway. Heavy footsteps were getting closer to my door. Then more hurried footsteps and shrill screams. *What the hell was going on outside?* Smoke came through the bottom of the door. I knew that I couldn't move. The smoke could be a diversion to get me out of my hiding space. The red dot was still looking for me around the room. I couldn't risk it, I had to stay put. I hoped that the footsteps outside my door was from someone who could rescue me.

I heard shouting from outside and doors slamming. Voices, male voices were yelling to the old couple down the hall. I heard the word, "Fire," but everything was muffled. It's hard to hear in the hallway when you're crouched down in your kitchen. Then I heard footsteps run to my door; pounding and shouting. My eyes went to the door.

The voice sounded firm and soft not as masculine and deep as James. "Hello in there. Do you hear me? This is the Fire Department. There's a fire in the building. Everybody out. Do you hear me?" he repeated.

Yeah, I did but I couldn't move. Death by gunshot or by fire. Great choices. I don't know how I finally found my voice, but I did. And surprisingly, it wasn't wavering as I thought it might. It was slightly panicked but strong.

"Hi. My name is Laura. I'm still in here. There's no fire here and hardly any smoke. I can't come out though. There's someone shooting at me through the window. I'm hiding behind a stupid refrigerator. I can't move from here. My place is riddled with bullet holes." There was silence for a bit. I suppose they had to think about something. Maybe they didn't believe me, but I wasn't lying. I know you don't believe me either, but it happened.

I watched the red dot move into the living room to right in front of me. It was too close. I'd never make it. The distance from the kitchen to the front door was too far. I'd need time to run it. Seeing that there was still no response from my supposed rescuers, I shouted at the firemen. "Slip a mask under the door so I won't inhale so much smoke. I'll run out when I can. I promise. This is how you can help me."

Another man spoke with a gruffer voice. "Let us in and we'll help you." His tone sounded like he thought I was a petulant child throwing a fit. Much like you'd say when someone is having a psychotic break. Is that the term for it, doctor?

I tried to plead with them to see reason. There was no point in us all dying. I was on the second floor. There were more people to save. They couldn't die trying to save me. "No. Listen to me. Why won't you listen? There's no way to save me. The only way is to do as I ask. He'll kill you if you come in." Another long uncomfortable silence. I figured these firemen were morons and it was a lost cause until one of them spoke up.

The first man spoke again, this time in a frustrated tone. " OK lady, here's the mask. We'll call the police and get help." I heard murmurs from them as he slid the mask under the door. They were probably talking about me. Calling me names like people do, saying I'm crazy and I'm not. I just got too close, I know too much, and James had to get rid of me. He's probably a professional killer. A man like that knows how to cover his tracks. He's probably long gone by now, onto the next town, the next gullible woman. But unlike his other victims, I'm not dead. I'm the girl who survived.

Yeah, I know, back to the story. I waited for a while. I was coughing from the smoke that continued to seep in under the door. I knew it was bad. I knew I had to move. I put my sleeve over my mouth as a makeshift mask, so I wasn't breathing in so much smoke. I waited, watching the red dot with singular preci-sion. Nothing else mattered but that red dot. When it finally moved down the hall to my bedroom, I knew this was my one and only chance. I ran and dove for the mask, the firemen left by the door and ripped open my front door. I didn't even bother to close it, I just ran out. I heard gunshots behind me. They spurred me on to run fast down the stairs. I felt a pain in my arm but kept going. I gripped the handrail for dear life as I sped down the steps. I heard the stairwell door to the fifth floor open just as I got to the ground floor. I ran even faster out of the stairway and into the hallway of my building. My doorman wasn't there. I saw a crowd of people outside and ran out to join them. I was free, breathing fresh air, looking up at the building that was partially in flames.

I saw firemen talking to a group of my neighbors, but the voices were garbled for some reason. I couldn't make out what anyone was saying. Was it a clinical delusional state, was it fear, was it a heightened adrenaline response? Was I injured? I don't know. I don't exactly remember this with crystal clarity. Memories are sometimes fuzzy like that. All I know is that the muted sounds were agitating me and made me even more aware of my surroundings. I looked up at my complex counting the windows and it looked like the fire started on the fifth floor right next to or in his apartment. He started it to get me out, so he could kill me.

It was a long time before my breathing returned to normal. One thought haunted me -- that James, the man who was kind and gentlemanly, had rigged this whole fire in the building just to kill me. I hugged myself and took deep breaths which worked to calm me down until I saw James out of the corner of my eye watching me at the end of the block in a fireman's costume. His eyes were dark and held no kindness in them. Was he always like this and he just pretended with me earlier? Why was he just standing there? No one seemed to notice him. But I wasn't imagining him. He was there. He was there. There was a fire, everyone could have just been thinking about themselves and not focused on looking around at faces. Doesn't prove anything. I opened my mouth to scream but nothing came out.

One second later, I was on the cold ground with warm blood all around me. Was I injured before? I felt a pain in my arm, could've gotten grazed by a bullet. Everyone was talking all at once now. I couldn't make out any of their faces. They all strangely blended into one. For all I know, I died, and you could be my version of Hell trying to convince me I'm crazy. Maybe I hit my head running out of my apartment? Maybe I died?

My eyes felt heavy and my body was weak. You'd say I fainted and was imagining this. But I wasn't, damn it! There was a small group of firemen talking about me real close thinking I was knocked out or dead or something.

"Looks like an accident somehow. I don't know why people aren't more careful."

"Where did it start?"

"I think it started in that empty apartment, 5E. Funny thing is we saw petals from flowers, lilies and something else by the kitchen window. The Super has no idea where they came from. He swears no one lives there."

"Weird. Thankfully we got all the tenants out just in time."

"A fire in summer, isn't that funny? It's already so hot."

"Terrible, Jimmy. Stop with the maudlin jokes, will ya?"

"Hey guys. You know that lady that was hiding behind a fridge?"

"Dude, how could I forget that?"

"Well, her place is destroyed but I couldn't find one bullet. Bullet holes but no bullets. Checked with the landlord, no new tenants in months."

"Wow, that's creepy. Let's get the little lady to the doctors." I froze when I heard that term and stared into the eyes of the fireman. He turned toward me whispering in my ear as he picked me up into his arms and carried me to the ambulance. "Clever girl hiding like that. Are you sure I ever existed? Have you any proof? Are you sure you know what's going on here? Are you sure you know where you are and where you're going?"

That was all he said as he put me in the back of the ambulance and waved, his dark eyes following me down the street. He was talking to the other firemen. He was having a conversation so this time other people saw him. I'm not crazy. Why won't you believe me? You really are the Devil, aren't you? Is this Hell? Am I dead? Did he convince you I was crazy?

Anyway, I passed out for a long time and woke up here in this hellhole of a looney bin. Eating stale food, you wouldn't give to prisoners. So, there's my story. I told you, I'm not crazy. Was that the story of a crazy person? You all should know that I'm going to figure out what's really happening. And then you and James will pay dearly for ruining my life. Just you wait. I'm coming for the both of you.

———————

ELEVEN

All Hallows' Eve

I sit at my window counting the days until All Hallows' Eve, the day when everyone dresses up in costumes, not really knowing anything about the magic this day holds. I was like that, too, when I was a child. I dressed up in pumpkin suits and superhero costumes but now, I don't need a costume. I don't need to pretend, or ward off the dead. I'm no longer afraid of the spirits that roam the earth. I don't need to become someone else. Halloween, for me, is the only time I ever really feel like me.

I cross off the days on my calendar with my favorite ballpoint pen until I see with excitement that Halloween is right around the corner. Tomorrow, in fact. I fix up my room until every dust particle is banished. I pick out the most gorgeous, sexiest outfit I ever bought, and prepare it for the next day.

As soon as daylight comes, I run as fast as my legs can carry me. I slow down only when I see him and he's just as I remember him. He stands there outside of his former home, watching through the window as his sister helps his elderly mother around the house. She makes his mother coffee and starts making eggs for the both of them. The smells from that kitchen are always bewitching. There is such a longing on his face. Fate has been quite cruel to my beloved.

I look at him and remember all the times we had together. I remember the first time we met in Pre-K and the wonderful drawings we made on the windows just to drive our teachers crazy. I can see us in first grade laughing at the first cuts and scrapes we got. I can see us climbing trees to read together in fourth grade. I remember the feel of his lips on mine when he kissed me for the first time in high school. I can see us on my bed, clear as day, a plate of cookies on the nightstand as we argued over colleges.

I see all the happy times that I wish I could relive again. I see them replaying in my mind like a film. I wish I could go back and enjoy them more, maybe change things, small things, in the hopes that I would have a longer future with him, that I could fix fate. But such things are not possible.

Life was so peaceful, so simple. We were naive and in love with no idea of the evil around us. We thought we'd have forever together. Apparently, the universe had other plans.

I move closer to him. Though my feet make a sound on the ground, leaves crunching under my boots, he makes no sign that he knows I'm there. I sigh heavily as I stand behind him. His mother and sister look so peaceful, sitting there in their small kitchen, eating and reading the newspaper.

I turn to him, and grab both of his hands in mine. He turns towards me slowly, with so much love in his eyes. It's as if my touch has awakened his desire, dragging him from his painful reverie. He disconnects his hands from mine to cup my face as he gently places his lips upon mine. Slowly, he deepens the kiss, making sure his feelings for me are clear. Everything we are, everything we feel for each other is in that kiss.

When we disconnect, my breathing is ragged, his lips are quivering, and his eyes are filled with tears, as are mine. We hold each other as the wind whips around us, throwing leaves against our clothes. We hold each other, content to just be in the moment, so happy to see each other after so long.

As much as we would love to stay this way, we disconnect a moment later and simply hold hands. We don't want to have to explain anything to the people in that house. They would never understand. My explanation would only bring his mother pain. So we leave before we're discovered.

We catch a movie, an indie horror film. He always loved those. And Halloween is the perfect time for horror films. There's always a fun festival happening somewhere. He holds me, knowing the supernatural usually makes me nervous and afraid, at least the way ghosts are portrayed in movies. Ghosts in real life are more tragic and loving than the scary, angry ones in films, all jealous of the living. Real ghosts aren't jealous, just sad at their fate.

After that, we go to our usual diner to catch up on things. No matter how many new stores open up, the dinner is always there. It's a constant fixture in the city I grew up in. It looks the same as it had a year ago. It's made up to look like a 1950's diner. The waiters all wear period clothing. It's actually quite fun and the food is delightful.

I know it's weird for me to come in wearing a fancy dress, but I could care less what people think. I don't bother myself with conventions since this isn't a conventional relationship. I feel the need to make myself look beautiful and that's what this designer dress does. It hugs my curves and makes me feel confident. I can tell by the way his hungry eyes roam over my figure, that he, too, likes this dress.

I tell him about my classes and how my family is doing. I show him the stories I wrote, the book I published. I tell him about the days when I feel like I can't go on because he isn't by my side making everything worthwhile. And I tell him about the days I love life and want to live forever. I try to fit an entire year into a couple of hours, I try to sum up a year's worth of machinations and desires.

We never leave before dessert. I love seeing his face light up as he eats a slice of pie, always cherry pie. This time, it's so good it makes him moan. My eyes flash with excitement at seeing him so happy.

Afterwards, we walk over to my place and we lie in each other's arms, content to feel each other's bodies. Sometimes we just hold each other, other times, we make love.

We always love to play games whether it's a video game or a board game. Clue is a personal favorite of ours. He is a very good guesser and such a challenge to beat.

Then we have an "artists' hour," as we like to call it, when I write a short story, inspired by our love and he writes a love poem, so beautiful it brings tears to my eyes.

I bring him up to speed on the new bands I like, and we dance energetically. The beat fuses through our bodies and urges us to move our feet.

Here with him, on this day, I'm free of the stress daily life inflicts on me, free from prying judgmental eyes, with just my love.

His curiosity sometimes brings him to my college and we attend a night class together. He says he's auditing the class. This year, it's a psych class. He actually enjoys it so much, he takes notes. He would have been a great student, given the chance. He has such a thirst for knowledge.

He's happy to get the chance to see where I go to school and suss out the other students. I was on a different campus this year. He loves my university.

We even wandered into a college Halloween party. We didn't wear costumes. Every other day of the year, I have to hide him, our relationship, have to wear a mask of normalcy. This is the one day I can just be, no masks required.

We look around the room at all the costumes around us, smiling at each other. He holds me in his arms and kisses my forehead. We don't say anything, we don't need to, just content to be together again.

We go out on the town in my car, talking and feeling the breeze running through our hair. We feel like a couple again.

The day always goes by so quickly. We always manage to fit in so many activities, but it never feels like enough.

I glance down at my watch and notice that we only have an hour left. Salty tears fall down my cheek at the prospect of having to say goodbye again. The goodbye is what kills me every time. My tears blur my vision for a few seconds as I'm reminded of the situation, of our "relationship." I wanted him to be around to love me, to marry me, to father my children. I knew that he was my soulmate and that I would not love again after him. Every man I meet pales in comparison. I know this relationship is difficult, unusual even, but we make it work.

We looked at each and knew it was time. I arrived at the cemetery. A large field of graves in front of us, like harbingers of doom. The cemetery felt oppressive and cruel at this hour, as it always did when we had to say goodbye.

I park the car and we slowly get out. A few minutes is all I have left. We kiss each other like it's the last time we'll ever see each other, desperation and so much love poured into the kiss.

He always tells me the same thing. He cups my face and forces a smile on his. He tries to make me smile. He hates seeing me upset. "Don't fear, my beloved. I will be back again. It's always difficult parting from you. But I will see you again, next year, when the veil between the living and the dead is thinnest."

A sad smile forms on my face. "Yes, till next time, my beloved."

"No one loves like we do. Our love is forever, stronger than death itself. Nothing can keep you from me. This is not a goodbye, no, this is I'll see you soon."

The corners of my mouth turn up in a small smile.

"You look gorgeous when you smile. I love you so much."

"And I you."

He looks at me intently, regret flashing on his face, momentarily. "Are you sure you want to wait for me? I refuse to 'move on,' whatever that means. You are everything to me and I would love to continue this with you, but is it fair for a ghost to ask for such a commitment? I had a chance, a life with you, and fate pulled us apart."

I run to him cupping his face, my fingers touching his solid skin, knowing soon he won't be corporeal anymore. "I chose this. You didn't force me. I would rather live one day a year with you then phone it in for some guy I settled for, just to live a normal life. I love you and I will take you anyway I can get you."

He smiles at me before he kisses my forehead. I try to pull him into a last kiss, but my hands go through him.

He smiles a wistful smile.

"Till next year," he calls out, darkness all around us.

"Till next year," I call out watching him walk to his grave. He smiles at the flowers I always leave by the headstone. His favorite line of poetry under his name and the year of his death. I touch the cold stone lovingly. I would see him again in a year.

"Nothing can stop our love," I say confidently, sure he can hear me. The night air is quiet, a half moon is out. I wrap my belt tightly around my coat as I leave the cemetery, having to don a mask again. A mask that explains why I never date and have no boyfriend. A mask that explains my perpetual disgust with men and why I keep to myself, having no friends. A mask to explain the inner turmoil swirling in my eyes, the stress that manifests in so many ways. A mask to hide the truth of our love.

"See you next Samhain, my beloved," I say as I drive away from the cemetery towards my other life.

TWELVE

You've Got to Be Kidding Me

Nikki hated Mondays like no one else she knew, but this was one for the books! It was like the universe was out to get her or something. Working late in this run-down 50s-style diner, a weird shadowy figure was staring at her from across the street. The way those eyes bore into her, she felt like she was at a peepshow.

Nikki had a long shift yet again. Do other people out there work from 7am-1am? To make matters worse, she couldn't leave until these drunks did. And they didn't seem like they were leaving anytime soon. *Great.*

Of course, her boss had left her alone to close shop. Oh yeah, leave the 19-year-old girl who looks even younger to close up the restaurant at 1am. That's not creepy or dangerous -- especially with the peeper out there. Nikki tried to reason with her boss, but he wasn't hearing it. He told her to do it or she was fired and hell, she needed the money to pay her rent so that ended the argument. He left with a self-satisfied smirk that Nikki was dying to smack off his face. She was so pissed. He left early because he wanted to take his lady love to dinner behind his wife's back. Can you believe that? *Really?!*

The entire night Nikki had the misfortune of dealing with horny assholes, trying to palm her ass while they ordered. Oh boy, did she want to break their arms. At times like these, she was reminded of her mother telling her that life was a series of compromises. Her mother didn't exactly mean being sexually objectified, serving pathetic men in a diner, but it fits. Nikki had to swallow so much just to survive in this job, just to get by. This couldn't be worth it. This wasn't really living.

She had never really clicked with her other colleagues. They had kids and husbands and responsibilities while Nikki was unattached. The way they said the word "unattached," it was as if it were the holy grail. What was so great about being unattached with no strings? It was awfully lonely from where Nikki was standing. By their reasoning though, Nikki could leave this job if she wanted. She had her whole life ahead of her. As if any of that was her fault. If they didn't like their life, why the hell didn't they change it? Why blame Nikki? And Nikki hated her life, too.

Of course, during her shift, she dropped some dishes. That was going to be taken out of her pay. *Fantastic.* She then proceeded to burn herself carrying a very hot plate to one of the customers. *Even better.* The cook was supposed to warn her it was hot. He probably didn't because…well, she had spurned his advances. *Yep. This job was Hell itself.* And to make matters worse, no one gave her a tip. The *whole* night. Not one lousy tip. *Like hello! If you're gonna feel a girl up all night, at least give her a tip. What the hell? Weren't they aware that waitresses lived off their tips? I mean seriously, isn't that common knowledge?*

The other waitresses got tips. Nikki wasn't exactly sure if they took her tips, thinking that she didn't really need the money. They had done that before. "Your parents could help you out," they said. Of yeah? That's why she was living alone in a studio, right!? In a sketchy part of town, no less. And why couldn't their friends or family help them out? Again, how was that Nikki's fault? *Damn this job.*

The cook left at midnight and so did one of the other waitresses, leaving Nikki alone with the grade A bitch, Sheryl. Sheryl would be leaving in a few minutes while Nikki had to stay till closing. *Wonderful.*

So that was the day she was having. *Fucking fantastic, right?*

Yeah, well, what about these drunks who refused to leave. Nikki actually threatened to call the cops. She'd had enough of this shit. But she didn't notice that the shadow moved closer to the window of the restaurant, obviously intrigued by her toughness. "Look, get your damn asses out of this fucking restaurant. It's beyond closing time. Go NOW!"

"Fucking bitch you can't-."

"Excuse me? Damn right, I *am* a bitch to men who leave no tip and feel me up every chance they get. I'm not some fucking blow up doll. I'm not a prostitute. I'm a waitress! You know what? I'm too good for this shit! I do need the rent but not this badly. You're right, Sheryl, have fun closing."

Nikki opened the door and walked out into the darkness. Walking out on that horrible job, the future in front of her. She heard her name being called but she didn't care. She'd had enough. She had wanted to leave for months, and tonight she just did it. It felt so freeing to just leave.

Of course, it was raining, and Nikki had no umbrella. There was one in the employee closet also called the "break room." *Ha. Some room.* Nikki was definitely not going back for the umbrella. Just her luck, but it was okay. It was just a little water. Nothing could ruin the high she was on. She was free. No idea how she would pay next month's rent, but that was next month's worry.

Nikki wished she had worn comfier shoes, but oh well. Her heels tapped on the cobblestone streets that led to her apartment. It was chilly out, and she hoped she wouldn't get pneumonia. It had been warmer at 6 AM when she woke up, but this threadbare sweater wasn't much protection against a strong wind and a torrent of rain.

Nikki pulled the collar up on her waitress outfit to combat the biting wind, when she heard a rustle behind her. She turned around but saw nothing. *"Probably one of those damn jerks from the freakin' restaurant,"* she thought to herself.

Nikki passed a car, and looked in the rearview mirror, only to see a shadow shaking its head. *Oh shit. It heard me? How could a figure hear my thoughts? What the ever-living fuck?*

Nikki looked behind her again but saw nothing there. Was this all in her head? Or was something following her? She started to get a bit scared and picked up the pace to her home. It was only three more blocks, she could make it. He couldn't be *that* close. He was a block, a block and a half behind her last time. Whatever it was couldn't be right behind her now.

Nikki slowly looked behind her, only to suddenly see a figure running towards her. How did it get that close? She wasn't looking in front of her and tripped over the cobblestones. Her body flew forward, the heel of her shoe got stuck in the space between two cobblestones, her ankle landing awkwardly. *Great a sprain. Perfect.* Her hands instinctively reached out, so her face was unmarred, but her arms were scratched to bits. Nikki's purse went flying along with her keys.

She swallowed hard knowing that she was the stupid girl in the horror movie and the guy was right behind her, ready to off her at any moment. *What a wonderful end to a wonderful day!* Her breathing picked up as she slowly turned her head to assess the danger only to find that yet again, nothing was there. Weirdly enough, the night had become silent. No chirps from any birds, no sounds of the rain, no sounds of the wind. Everything was just silent. When is the night ever silent? It was as if a monster had eaten the noises around her.

Nikki quickly grabbed her bag and staggered forward. She was so shaken, her feet weren't really prepared to carry her home quite yet, not to mention her sprained ankle. But there was no room for rest, not with whatever was following her. He would come back soon. She had to run.

She used the banister on the stairs to her neighbor's house to balance herself, as she slowly stood up and grabbed her keys. Nikki saw something approaching on her left. It was a balloon. A silver balloon. It was traveling quite quickly over to her. Faster than any balloon she'd ever seen. The second it reached her face, it stopped and hovered there. Then a second later, it popped loudly and suddenly. She screamed as shreds of rubber and blood, so much blood, splashed onto her face and uniform.

Nikki turned to see the glint of a knife in the distance. She heard heavy footsteps behind her approaching her quickly. She screamed out into the night knowing that no one would hear her. Everyone was likely asleep by now with their window closed to keep out the heavy rain.

She was all by herself. That fact didn't stop her from screaming again just in case a passerby was around.

Nikki ran the two blocks to her apartment, running through the pain in her ankle. Behind her, the streetlights went out soundlessly. You'd think there would be sparks and the sound of breaking glass but there was nothing. It was as if they were snuffed out like a candle.

A shadow fell over her, engulfing her figure, towering over the buildings beside her. His footsteps were even, steady. He wasn't running anymore. He suddenly seemed in no rush to stab Nikki to death. *Good to know.* She was still running.

Why hadn't she just called in sick today? She had one more block to go. Nikki started throwing random things at him. Yeah, it sort of slowed her down but it slowed him down more. *Goal achieved.* Nikki was quite ungraceful and haphazard about throwing items but hey, if it works, don't knock it.

She found a broken umbrella someone discarded on the street and chucked it at him. The creature made an "oomph" and stopped walking for a moment. OK, that was a little absurd, but beggars can't be choosers. She spilled the garbage can onto the sidewalk making quite a mess in her wake. She threw dog poop at him, fighting the urge to laugh as it splattered onto her would-be attacker. She found empty beer bottles on the ground that she threw at him and one of them broke on the creature. *Score.* "Take that, freaky clown!" Nikki yelled. She wasn't sure it was a clown, she hadn't seen his face, but hey, balloon equals clown, usually right? Good enough guess.

Whatever it was let out a bone-chilling scream and lunged for her. Nikki dove out of the way and channeled all her anger at her life, her crappy, meaningless job, the frustration at having to find a new one, her so-called, slightly judgmental friends, her small, cramped apartment -- everything into that shove. Nikki managed to shove the whole garbage can at the shadow. There was so much velocity behind her throw that the garbage can, once it landed on him, rolled the shadow down the block. It made a series of horrifying sounds and screams, none of them human. It sounded like a scream from a bird mixed with the screech of a VCR rewinding backwards. Quite unnatural.

Nikki flung herself towards the door of her apartment building, desperately trying to get the keys into the lock. She screamed at the door, as she saw her attacker slowly get up. It started moving towards her. Nikki's hands shook from fear. With each passing second, it got closer. *Why wouldn't the keys go into the lock? Come on!*

Finally, she opened the front door, flung herself in, literally onto the floor and locked it behind her. *Why couldn't I live in a doorman building? The building supposedly has a video camera but the Super never turns it on. Really great security here.* The shadow pounded on the glass door, glaring angrily at her. Another second and it would have gotten in.

Wasting no time, she ran to the door of her apartment on the first floor. The second she got in, she breathed a sigh of relief and crumpled against the heavy door. She tried to catch her breath and calm down. *What the hell was that creature? And why was it chasing me? Could he break in eventually? Am I really safe here? I guess I could call the cops…and say what? A freaky shadowy clown is out to get me? Hello, rubber rooms."*

Nikki sighed heavily and turned on all the lights in her apartment. She sunk into her comfy couch and started to relax. Until she saw movement out of the corner of her eye. Something was moving by the window. A darkness fell over her apartment. She bolted up and turned towards the window.

The being's piercing eyes bore into Nikki's soul. The rain dripped down its now soaked form. It placed the knife it held in a death grip on the window, slowly scraping it, the message ominously clear.

When it spoke, it spoke in her mind, not using its mouth. Possibly because it had none. The tone of the voice was an unnaturally low pitch, full of menace. "Soon, you will be mine. This brick building will not keep me out. Enjoy your seconds of respite, *human.*"

The second he said that, the shadow drew away from her apartment slightly, revealing that the lights had been on the whole time, he was simply blocking the light. Nikki shivered at his words. The being gave a maniacal laugh at her growing fear. It was enjoying this. Nikki closed the blinds with a growl. She refused to be its victim, whatever it was. She had already given him too much of her fear. That ended now!

Why was he trying to kill her in the first place? Just because he was a mental case and she happened to be in the wrong place at the wrong time? Or was it hungry? Monsters don't exist so what was this? And where did it come from? It didn't look like it was in a talking mood, more like a killing mood.

Just at that moment the lights went completely out, silently. Nikki knew it wasn't a question of bulbs or fuses. This was the creature's doing.

Nikki was a victim to all these horrible people, bosses, and so-called friends. Now today, she chose her destiny and she chose not to die! How dare he determine what should happen to her! This was her life and while it may be a crappy one, it was still hers.

Nikki laughed at him from the door. He growled at her, trying desperately to open it. She quirked her eyebrow as she yelled, "Give it your best shot, honey."

Nikki walked away from the shadow at her door and walked into her room. She slowly peeled off her wet waitress uniform, shivering in her room. She felt a surge of cold air and then a loud pounding. Nikki heard glass break, and then felt a whoosh of cold air, enough to cause goosebumps over her arms and legs.

Nikki watched as a puff of smoke dove right past her. The sheer force of it knocked her down. Thankfully, she just fell back onto her bed.

Her closet door jiggled and rattled against the frame, until the door opened slowly, and the shadow materialized into one of her fears, a clown. The clown laughed at Nikki as it stepped out of the closet, its warm breath ghosting over her cheek, its eyes roving over her body.

Of course, Nikki *had* to be in her underwear for this. The creature couldn't have waited for her to change? It's not like she could fight effectively in a cold room with soaking wet clothes.

The clown chuckled at her before slowly dragging its knife across her face, not enough to cut her but enough to get the message across that it meant business.

"Such a pretty girl. I can smell your fear, little one, and it's delicious." The voice was so melodic, so entrancing, so soothing. Like a lullaby lulling Nikki to her death. But when it raised its arm to stab her, she laughed.

Nikki laughed at it. She'd had enough. Life was so much scarier than he was. Sure, he gave her a good scare, but she refused to die. She refused to give him the energy he needed to survive. She took back her fear and laughed. "Sorry honey, but with the day I've had, *please*. You are the *least* scary thing in it. Fuck you!"

The clown was shocked. It thought it had her, but it could sense the shift. Nikki wasn't afraid anymore. Of all the victims it consumed, she was the one to destroy him.

The clown screamed as the closet reclaimed it. The clown was sucked back into the hell it came from. The knife clattered on the floor, as the clown's body was squished into a small black void, until it ceased to exist.

Nikki picked up the knife and smiled, placing it on her nightstand as a badge of honor, a testament to the day she fought back against the universe and won.

Nikki slept soundly that night only too happy to think about waking up to her new life, to a new and stronger Nikki. To a future full of possibilities knowing now that whatever the universe threw at her, she could take it. She was stronger than she thought, and no one would subjugate her again, not creepy-ass clowns or crappy-ass bosses. Tomorrow would be awesome.

———————————

THIRTEEN

Christmas with the Devil *erotica*

C hristmas Eve already? Time sure does go by fast. Wasn't I supposed to visit the Devil in his penthouse two weeks ago? Oh well, I'll be there soon enough. As if I ever do anything on *his* schedule. He must really love me. Damn right he does -- he'd be a fool not to. I'm a Hell of a catch, pun intended, dear. I'm the one woman in all eternity who refuses to put up with any crap, even from the Devil himself. And I must say that even though I run cons and do side jobs and such to keep a girl interested, you know -- not that Hell is boring, but it's fun to have hobbies -- I co-run Hell fantastically. Accept no substitutes. The Devil has no idea how much work I do behind the scenes to make it the wonderful hellish vision it is today. So of course that level of perfection gives me the freedom to do as I please and sometimes that means coming late. *C'est la vie.* I look absolutely ravishing. Should make up for lost time, always does.

I had to go off on a job. I was getting a tad restless as the Creative Director. I had to switch it up a little. I miss Hell and my sweetie, though. Hope he's doing awesome. I'll see him soon enough. I can just see us sitting there by the fireplace and snuggling, a dead human or demonic guard at our feet. Our meetings always end in someone's death. I can imagine his strong arms wrapping around me from behind, the warm blood splatter blanket he loves so much around my shoulders, his soft lips kissing the back of my neck. He leans in to whisper that I'm his, as if I'd ever forget. And I catch a whiff of his cologne. Cigar smoke, whiskey, musk, and a campfire in the deep woods, all combined into an undeniable scent that he wears so well. It's masculine, intense, dark and so very devilish. Oh boy, I'm getting all hot and bothered just thinking about him. I've got it bad even after all these centuries.

Oh wait, it's the holidays. Oh, crap. I need a present! And there goes the warm and fuzzy feelings. Goodbye lustful thoughts and hello holiday shopping. Damn it. Okay, well I gotta think big for a present. I mean it's for THE Devil. I have to go big or darkly romantic. Hmm…choices, choices. I wonder what he's getting me? What would I, the Creative Director of Hell and all-around-best-assassin and thief actually need? I already have the love of the Devil himself. Yeah, now I really am wondering, what he got me. Oh well, I'll just have to wait and see.

I feel liquid hit my shoe and I look down and yeah, I totally stepped in blood. Talk about a ruined moment. Such a rookie move. Hello… these *are* my favorite shoes. Okay, they *were*. Wonderful. Try explaining that stain to the cleaners or shoe repair. I only just bought them, uh about two months ago. Can't return them now and these were pricy. I know you're thinking dead body, blood, stop talking about fashion but fashion matters, people, remember that. Image matters, especially for the Creative Director of Hell Inc.

I sighed heavily as my attention turned to the dead body at my feet. A darkly ingenious idea came to me. "Hmmm. You know you're one lucky stiff. You may prove to be even more useful." I got rid of the remains quickly and without any further injury to my clothes, I'm happy to report. I teleported to the shore to await my handler. Yes, even the Devil's lover, girlfriend -- we don't do titles, so *human* those titles -- yes, even I have a handler.

I love being at the shore. It's so relaxing watching the tide come in, so very natural, the ebb and flow like life itself. It always calms me. I breathed in the salt air and just relaxed for a moment. Hell's business was frenetic, souls always needing something, paperwork always piling up, ads to approve, the work never stops. But now I could just be in the moment, the wind in my hair. The only way it would be better is if the Devil were here with me.

I should probably get the show on the road. I slowly look at my watch and see that it's high time I called Jackson, my handler, for an update. I do believe he owes me money.

My frustration grows with how long it's taking him to answer. Seven rings already and he still hasn't picked up. I'm about to lose hope and I start to plan his murder when he answers on yes, the eighth ring. *Oh no, don't rush on my account dear. I'm only the co-ruler of Hell, take your time, it's all good. Cue the sarcasm.* Jackson's really pushing it today.

"After the eighth ring, really? You're lucky I didn't just hang up and come over, just teleport right there in your living room."

There's a distinct moan in the background. *Real tacky Jackson. Put it back in your pants. If he weren't one of the most capable demons (at least when it comes to deals, murder, and mayhem, which is all that counts as a demon), I would have killed him a long time ago.*

"Well, hello there, darling."

Oh no! He did not just get all flirty with me! I'm taken, moron! Disgusting pig and she moaned again? In the name of everything evil, what the friggin' hell is wrong with him! I need a coffee and better minions.

"This isn't a damn social call. I'm not that kind of girl, honey. I'm the assassin type remember? And with the Devil, surely you remember him, right? Now where's my money?"

"And proof of delivery?" he asks real tentative, knowing he has to cross his T's and dot his I's but making me angry is one thing nobody wants. So he's not a complete idiot.

"Proof of delivery, really? That's the euphemism we're going with? You mean the stiff, right? You have a picture on your phone. I am a professional. If you stop having sex with her for a moment, you could look at it. I'll wait."

"What-"

Oh man. He acts shocked. Classic. Really Jackson?

"I'm not deaf. Unless you moan in a high-pitched voice, that's not you. Now where is the damn money? You know I'm not a patient woman. Don't make me ask you again."

"Hold on, Mindy. Hold on. I know. I know. It's work. Wait a minute. Daddy will be right back, OK?"

And there goes my breakfast. As if I really needed that mental image. I'm going to literally have to kill someone again just to get that out of my head.

"Daddy really? It's 8 am -- way too early for that."

Jackson refuses to answer, a wise man. There's silence on the other end and what sounds like shuffling. Good he got up and he's looking at his text, one would assume. That or he's walking to the bathroom.

"Oh yes, I see it. OK. Wait, why is his heart missing?"

Like I haven't taken a body part before? And now he starts to notice?

"It doesn't matter. It was post mortem. And that's my business He's dead. MONEY!"

"I'm coming over."

"Let me make this clear. I have business with the Devil, business I can't be late for, happening later on today. Don't make me late by giving me my money late. You got it? You get here in twenty minutes!"

"Coming right now, my Queen."

Suck up. That's the first time he's ever called me Queen. Not going to say it didn't work but he is totally a suck up.

I teleport back to my apartment and quickly clean up a bit. No sense letting him in on just how frisky the Devil and I can be. A girl's gotta have some mysteries.

Jackson comes promptly in twenty minutes, like a good boy. But he came over without a shirt. Not sure if that was on purpose or if he got so waylaid with … Mandy, Mindy, was it, she wouldn't let him go and he didn't have time to put on a shirt? Sigh!

My eyes rake over his body. Not bad but nowhere near as amazing as the Devil's body. Pure sin that one. And hey, you can't blame a girl for looking. It's a guy with his shirt off. Who doesn't look at that?

Jackson opens his mouth, probably to say something lascivious no doubt. But I shut it down quickly and take the money offered, nearly pushing him out the door. I don't have time for his antics. My darling Devil is waiting and neither of us has any patience.

I walk over to the kitchen and open up my oven. Demons don't eat and I don't cook so it's the perfect place to hide the money. Truth be told, I have money hidden in almost every city in the world, a girl can never be too careful.

Now I can put my attention back to where it's needed, the Devil's gift. I wrap his present and put it in a cooler which I have labeled, Blood Donation, O-. That way no pesky humans will deter me from the task at hand.

I can't wait to see him. And play all those delicious games. He's so very good at being dominant and I love to submit to his wicked little mind. Mmhmm. This time apart has been rough. Hmm. On both of us. I bite my lip as a flurry of heated images come into my mind. I smile before walking out the door with a small bookbag and my cooler.

I get on the bus at 9 am. Perfect. I should get there at the projected time. He told me he needed time to get things ready so why not do traveling the human way. See how our constituents, so to speak, travel. I slowly take out my phone and cycle through some fun, "darkly inclined" songs about dark love, psychosis and murder. Music really does get one in the mood.

I choose a seat by the window, so I can watch the landscape change. Simple joys really. I let my mind wander as I enjoy the moment on this uncomfortable seat next to man who is squishing me into the window. But none of that matters. The journey should be enjoyed as an experience.

A few hours later and it's time to leave the bus. I brush my shoulders off and pull my leather collar up. Space -- what a nice concept that buses can't seem to understand. I'll need something else to get me the rest of the way there. Now, don't worry dear reader, a woman like me always has a plan.

I slowly, really slowly, and kind of sensually if I'm being honest, take my knife out from inside my pants. I flash it at a biker who dares to look at me. This body is mine and the Devil's. Fuck, the biker's wandering eye. He seems not to take that information well.

Can't blame him. I'd be upset, too, if I couldn't get this body. To make my murderous intent clear though, I throw the knife right by his head and then with super speed, I throw another in between his legs while he's moving. Hard to do but I can. Think with your dick, lose said dick. Makes sense to me.

The whole time he's been eying his bike so of course I get on that one. Then some guy starts touching me and trying to pull me off the bike. Not happening, idiot. I take a knife from my boot and chuck it at his head as a warning. A rather dangerous endeavor for HIM. No one touches me. Of course, I'd rather not drop ten bodies. I'd have to call the cleaners to make sure no evidence of me remained. That would be nice – the Creative Director of Hell on trial for killing ten…humans? Just what we need.

The man didn't have the good sense to leave me be. He actually had the gall to take the knife out of the wall and get ready to throw it at me. Well, that's it. They're going to die. The feeling is so strong to murder them all, I feel like I was choking. But I have to show restraint. I'm a high-ranking demon! Idiotic males, gotta love em'.

I drew my gun out from the front of my pants slowly, relishing the feel of cold metal against my lower stomach. Without even looking I aimed and shot his hand. "Next time big boy, know when to quit," I yelled back.

This motorcycle had a place to put my cooler and my bookbag. Perfect. I put the helmet on. I didn't want to get stopped by cops or given a ticket. Once on the open road I get aggressive, and impatient. I drive crazy and I like it like that. I constantly swerve in and out of traffic, bikes, people, cars. I even speed through a red light. It was taking too long to change. High-ranking demons can't be forced to abide by human traffic laws … how silly. I ride until I run out of gas.

I'm making good time. I'm only two hours away now. Just enough to finish up the small job I took on. I knew I'd be here in time. I'm a planner. Every hour, every mode of transport was already planned. I filled up the motorcycle a bit. I much prefer them to all other modes of transportation save teleportation. Teleportation is my favorite by far.

I walk over to the quaint little diner in this Podunk town I'm in. I slowly open the door that jingles when I do. I groan at that. Why don't I just paint an arrow over my head? So much for staying off the radar. People will remember a hot redhead in a leather jacket, especially in a town like this. Oh well. I quickly give the "greasy spoon" a once over. If not for my contact, I'd never walk into a place like this. I walk with my head held high ignoring the patrons and their lustful gazes as I walk to the back of the diner to meet with my contact. He wanted an occult item that I just so happen to have acquired last month at a demonic auction so this hand off was an easy job to do. The second I sat down the waitress came. Funny because I didn't see her anywhere. It's like she magically appeared. I looked intently into her eyes only to see that she was a demon.

"Muriel."

"Lilith," she whispered.

"Heavens to Betsy, darling. Does the big bad have you working here?

"I actually like it, Lil. You can't imagine how many deals I close. Truckers can be awful friendly to a pretty face and small towns are filled with wishful people. Not to mention the juicy gossip."

"To each his own, darling. It's good to see you. I'm seeing the boss soon so, I'll tell him hi from you."

"Of course. Thank you, my liege. You look gorgeous as always."

"You flatterer! Well, I have to get the show on the road. Can't be late and all. Can I have a warm cherry pie?"

"Coming right up," Muriel said with a smile.

I wait until Muriel goes in the back to turn to my contact.

"You picked this place because of Muriel?"

"Do you have the item?"

Rude much? Would it kill you to small talk with me?

"I'm the Creative-."

"Forgive me. We're both just in a rush."

Oh ok. Fuck you too.

"Fine. Fine. Here it is. Now where is my occult item? The one our boss is desperately looking for?" Lilith inquires.

The squirrely man, what was his name? David, I think, opens

his small briefcase confirming he does have it. Would really love to know how he got his hands on that. We make a little switch and he's off on his merry way. The cherry pie is divine. I tip the girl well, she is one of ours after all, and leave the diner with a rare and powerful relic. All in a day's work.

I drive for a bit more and then dump the motorcycle in a ditch somewhere. I want to surprise my beloved, not make horribly loud motorcycle sounds. And besides, I stole it. Wouldn't want the cops to walk in on the things we do behind closed doors. I breathe in the cool air along with the wonderful emotions of the people around me. They are so sickeningly happy, so much holiday cheer. Sometimes, I rather hate being an empath.

I smile as I find carolers just up ahead. What a perfect way to say hello. I grab my cooler and my book bag and make my way over to them. I quickly make the musical score suddenly appear in my hands.

My high heels crunch the snow beneath my feet, making my presence known to all in a couple of steps. I walk confidently up to the group and speak in a meek and passive voice. Talk about a wolf in sheep's clothing.

"Hello, fellow carolers. I am so sorry to intrude, but I was wondering if you could find it in your hearts to allow me to sing with all of you. I would love to bring the Christmas spirit to all of these people. The group I was with earlier disbanded and I'm here all alone."

"Oh, of course. I'm so sorry. No one should be alone on the holidays."

"I couldn't agree more."

And soon I'll be naked by a fireplace with a fierce, evil being on top of me. And you all will probably be dead. If they only knew.

I fought the urge to vomit and plastered on a fake smile as I pretended to sing as we went from door to door. Why humans liked to freeze their asses off singing to strangers all the while getting nothing in return, was beyond me. I see no appeal in doing this. And the singing was just okay. I think someone was flat in the back and it wasn't me.

As soon as we got to the gates of the last, huge house, the very house of the Devil himself, I started a new con. How did I know which one was his house? The one he moved into just yesterday? Hello, empath here. I could sense demons by the gate. How do I not know where my lover lives? He prefers not to tell me exactly which house. We like playing games with each other. And it seemed, judging by the large number of demonic guards, I'd have to play a game to get in. I guess the Devil doesn't care about these demons because my games always turn bloody.

The carolers walk up to the front gate. The overly friendly caroler waves to the camera, beaming. *What a moron! First one to die, I'm sure.*

"Hi there. We're here to bring Christmas cheer."

I walk up and stand right behind her smiling maliciously into the camera. "Well, they are, I'm here to see the Devil. I think he's expecting me."

As one might predict, that brought the demons out. The boss loves to see me fight and I love to put on a show for my man. They don't stand a chance, mere demon extras. "Well, boys, are you just going to menace or are we going to play?"

I kick the demon that opens the gate bringing him to the ground, where I quickly slit his throat. I wipe my special knife on my monogramed handkerchief -- would be quite foolish to get my leggings soiled. I always carry my monogramed handkerchief to wipe away any messes. Then I throw my knife at an oncoming demon, killing him instantly. Two down, brilliant.

"Feel free to kill these people. I need to talk to your boss, our boss. Die or move out of the way!" I yell over my shoulder. I pause for a moment and then look back at the carolers. "Or you all could make wishes and we'd be happy to give you everything you desire. It's the holidays after all. Isn't there something you want? Tell these nice gentlemen if there is. Safe passage for you if you do."

A demon tackles me to the ground. Like, really? I have so many knives it's not even funny. Yes, a girl can have knives and wear dresses, I'm living proof. I kill the demon and then retrieve my knives. I hear several carolers making deals. How lovely. I am quite the saleswoman, I know. I walk right into my beloved's house. I don't sense any other demons, they're all with the carolers. Good, we have the house all to ourselves.

I walk into the living room and see how beautifully decorated it is. There are Christmas lights all over the place and even a deco-rated Christmas tree in the corner. The room was covered with wood paneling and a lavish, plush, rather big, black sofa was in the center of the room. The ceiling had gold inlay. Oh, my, and that fireplace. Wait a minute is that a picture of me on the mantelpiece? I walk over to inspect it. The picture is such a sweet one. We're both laughing and gazing into each other's eyes.

I'm so distracted by this rather sentimental gesture that I don't notice that the Devil and one of his henchmen are in the room. Apparently said demon is not happy that I got past him to see the boss. The demon takes advantage of my distraction and in a matter of seconds has a knife to my throat. *That moron!*

I look over at my beloved to see that he's absolutely livid. His eyes are red, and his fist are balled at his sides. He is always quite possessive, which is what I love about him. He growls at the demon and I have to bite my lip to suppress a moan. I love seeing him agitated and fiery like this. Because when all the drama ends, he'll be rough and possessive and I love that.

I keep my movements fluid but quick and take out a knife and press it into his stomach. OK, not a kill shot, but I wasn't expecting another demon. Damn him and his games.

In my haste to get my knife in the demon's stomach, I dropped the present – well, the cooler. That's what you want - a broken present. Then again, I did add packing material and some buffers so there's a chance it will be OK.

"And what do you think YOU'RE doing?" he yells at his minion who is currently clutching his bleeding stomach.

"Protecting you, sir," he coughs out.

"From what? From Lilith? Do you see her trying to harm me?"

"But she killed-."

"I imagine they attacked first. Get YOU HANDS OFF HER! NOW! STEP AWAY."

The demon had the gall to take his hands off me and push me into the Devil's arms.

Hello, precious cargo here. Handle me with care, you gruff imbecile!

The Devil cups my face and speaks so gently to me. I sigh a happy sigh at having his hands on my cheeks, at finally seeing him after my long journey.

"You OK?"

"You, caring and loving? Hmm. Don't ever change dearest. I'm fine. Can't say the same for your demons but as you said, they attacked first."

He smiles warmly at me and kisses me on the forehead. I can tell by his heated gaze that he wants to do a lot more but not with demon number two over there. He slowly strides over to the demon and takes out my knife only to plunge it deeply into the demon's heart. I love watching my man kill. It really gets me going.

"No one touches Lilith, got it?" The Devil barks to the stray demons approaching him."

I'm gone for a bit on assignment and the new demons don't even know who I am? Ouch.

The demons back up and nod to him, locking the door to give us some privacy.

"Except the Devil himself, of course." I reply smirking.

"Such a cheeky little-."

"Careful dear with your next word choice. Besides you wouldn't have it any other way," I remind him.

He smirks at my comment as he usually does. I move away from him throwing him a seductive look over my shoulder as I walk around the room again knowing full well he's behind me, taking in my gorgeous dress and how it hugs my curves deliciously. I pretend to note this thing and that, paying attention to nothing in particular. I just love teasing him and making him wait for it. After a bit, I speak up.

"What an eventful little celebration. I should have expected nothing less. It was so fun seeing you get all worked up over little old me."

"You're my one and only girl. I love you, darling."

I whirl around beaming at my beloved. "Same here, handsome. Don't worry I won't tell. It would kind of ruin your rep for sure if your demons knew you had feelings. Or rather the full extent of your feelings. And on that note, here's a little present for you."

I walk across the room and slowly bend down giving him a little show as I carefully take out the wrapped present.

"It's a little sticky and bloody, but I'm sure you'll love it."

"My favorite kind of present."

"Usually mine too."

He gives me such a genuine and happy smile as he opens his present carefully. The second he sees what it is, he lets out a chuckle. I let out a sigh of relief that it's unbroken and unharmed.

I walk closer to him, wrapping my arms around his waist. "You have my heart, honey. I would have used my own but then I'd be dead, and dead isn't a good look on me. It's a heart from one of my targets."

"Always thinking of me, I see, even when you're working. That's so sweet darling. Here's something for you."

He spins me around easily and holds me in his arms, just as eager to touch me as I am to touch him. He reaches over and hands me a large, slightly moving package. I raise my eyebrows at him, but he simply steps back and motions me to open it. My face lights up instantly. I love surprises and presents so much. I never have a wish list for these sorts of occasions, so this was really a surprise. I open the box carefully and let out a squeal as I see what it is. A small scruffy adorable black puppy with big red eyes stares back at me curiously. The Devil gave me a dog!

"Cerberus had puppies?" I inquire. "I didn't know the old girl was pregnant."

"I made sure you didn't, would ruin the surprise if you did. She had a litter with a wolf dog she found when she was roaming the forest collecting a soul for me. She took a liking to him and mated to my disapproval and the puppy you're holding is one of their offspring, a girl to be exact. I do love the juxtaposition of something that appears to be cute but in reality, is anything but. I specifically chose the cutest one for you.

"I love that, too. And she's so adorable, my darling. I love her. Always a smooth operator."

"You're a strong, independent woman who wants her freedom and a chance to do her own jobs, pave her own way outside of Hell from time to time. But I don't like the idea of you going off on dangerous jobs given to you by my underlings. Not one bit and so in an effort to protect what's mine, I'm giving you Cerberus's daughter. This way I know you're protected everywhere you go and that you'll always come back to me in one piece. If it helps, think of the pup as backup."

"I wouldn't expect anything less from you, darling. I like the idea of being protected by you. Not that I need it."

"Mmhmm. It will grow into a medium sized dog. You can feed it whatever you like."

"Will it have powers?'"

"Hmm...well this is the first hellhound to mate with a dog, so I have nothing to base my assumptions on. All I can say is, maybe."

"That's quite a gift."

"Glad you like it. "

"How about I name her Artemis? I always did like mythology and Artemis protects women and the hunt. Apt don't you think?"

The Devil smiles broadly at my suggestion.

"Artemis it is. Now me and your mother have things to get to, Artemis. Shoo."

The dog promptly leaves through the dog door and waits by the demons stationed at the front door. I peek through the window and watch with delight as Artemis eyes the demons warily and growls, making the demons back away so the pup can stand at the center of the door. Artemis stands up straighter baring her teeth as a warning to anyone that would dare enter. She's already shaping up to be quite the guard dog. Good girl.

My liege brings my attention back to him as he pins me to the wall. I growl menacingly. It's all an act. I love when my King dominates but I'm Lilith and I wouldn't be me if I gave up so easily.

"Don't like being controlled even by me? My, my, aren't we feisty?"

"If you wanted otherwise you'd have sex with one of your underlings."

The Devil crashed his lip onto mine. Our tongues battle for dominance. His teeth graze my lips while I bit down on his. The Devil tastes blood. He pulls back, licks his lips and smiles darkly at me. He presses my body against the wall and bites and nibbles my neck. I keep trying to break free. At first to attempt to dominate him but now I just want to grab his head and position him where I really want him. After a moment, he lets me break free. Intriguing. I throw the Devil onto the couch by the fireplace. I rip off his shirt and mark his neck in return so his minions know he's mine.

"Now your demons will know who you belong to," I say seductively.

The Devil stares at me with lust-blown eyes. I slowly start a strip-tease motioning him to stay put on the couch. My leather coat is on the floor next to my scarf in seconds. I slowly strip off my dress edging it down my long legs. I step out of it giving him a great view of my ass. I toss the dress aside and then slowly strip my leggings down my legs as I look at him from between my legs. He makes a sound between a growl and a moan. I love getting him all worked up.

I take off his belt in one fluid motion. Then I aggressively pull down the Devil's pants. I take his belt and caress my nipples with it. I jerk at the tickling sensation against my now pert nipples. I close my eyes and really focus on how the leather feels against my soft skin.

The Devil desperately wants to throw me down and take me then and there. I can see it in his eyes. He grabs onto the arms of the couch for dear life in hopes that he can remain still. Now whose playing games, my beloved? He always seems to like mine.

I lick my lips and wink at him. I lean over making sure to give him a good view of my breasts as I use his belt to tie his hands together. "No touching until you're a good boy," I tell him. I hope he returns the favor when it's his turn to be dominant. I smirk as I slowly unzip his pants.

I grab his neck and kiss him passionately. My hand slowly starts to move up and down his newly freed cock. I can feel the tension in the kiss. My darling is losing patience. I love teasing him, I do, but I can't wait to see what he does next.

The Devil snaps his fingers and the belt dropped on the floor next to my jacket. He grabs my waist and presses his body into mine, holding me in place. He snaps his fingers twice, once to rid himself and me of the few articles of clothing we still had on, and once to teleport us to his bedroom. Once there, he quickly binds my wrists to the bedpost. How I secretly longed to be taken like this, to be dominated by the Devil himself. He admires his handiwork and noticed my delight at being bound. My chest rises and falls excitedly, my eyes watching his intently. They're filled with such mischief and longing. He watches the way the firelight dances across my naked body, so ready and willing to submit to my master. But alas, we must play his game. I have to pretend to be a little sad that I can't take over.

"Really darling, can't take a strong woman?"

"I love a strong woman as much as the next man, but this is different. I need you to know that you're mine."

"I already know that."

"We've been apart for a bit. You might have forgotten. I need to claim every part of you. I need to make fresh marks on your body. I need you to scream my name, so all my minions can hear who you belong to. I need you to remember that I care about you, I protect you. My demons give you jobs, you are the co-founder of Hell Inc., the most hard-working demon ever and I appreciate everything you do. But I'm the one who gives you pleasure. You are mine! I am the King of Hell and will not be trifled with. I will make you remember who you care about."

"Well, are you just going to talk about it?" I tease. Finally, the game is over. I can just submit to his desires. I can let him claim me yet again, remind me why I would never need any other lover.

The Devil walks with purpose and confidence towards me with a fierce look in his eyes. If I didn't know any better, I'd believe I was his prey. He gives me his characteristic smirk as he jumps on the bed, hovering over my naked body.

"Don't you look like a pretty picture? Good enough to eat."

"You promise?"

"If you're a good girl."

"Oh, honey, I'm always bad."

"We'll see."

"You know, I made a playlist on my phone, thought it might set the scene. It has the usual- murder, kidnapping, stalking, psycho lovers etc."

"Always the romantic."

My darling got off the bed and quickly retrieved my phone from my leather jacket. He laughed at some of the names of my playlists until he settled on "The Devil and Lilith Fun Times."

"Catchy name."

"I thought as much."

The Devil stalks over to me taking in every curve on my small frame. He grabs my neck tightly and forces his tongue down my throat claiming my mouth as his. He pushes me back against the bed, his chest holding me down. His fingers ghost over my body slowly making their way down to where I really needed them to go.

He slowly puts one finger inside me and starts moving in and out so slowly, reverently almost. He bends down to bite lightly on my nipple. I arch my back and try to move his finger or wiggle in any way, but the Devil wasn't having it.

He slapped me once, on the thigh, as a warning not to struggle and just lie there and enjoy it. I arch my eyebrow curiously at the display of dominance. Slapping me? Well, this was going to be a fun holiday for sure. The Devil caresses the place where he previous slapped and then slowly moves from one nipple to the other.

His hand slides back down to slowly enter my pussy, this time adding another finger and curling it just so. He drank in my moans and pleadings for more until he couldn't hold out anymore. He growled and stared intently at me signaling me that he couldn't wait any longer. He always let me know his intentions like the gentleman he was. I nodded that now would be quite fine. I felt the same way. I needed him inside me and didn't want to wait any longer. But like the gentleman he was, he needed me to come first.

He adds more fingers and moves faster inside me curling them all at the same time. I moan even louder. When he starts moving down to lick my clit, I really lose it and started shaking.

"Gonna come," I barely let out.

"By all means," he replies with a smirk.

That was all the encouragement I needed. I came screaming his name with such reverence even I was surprised. The Devil didn't let me come down off my high and instead, placed his cock all the way inside not a second later. You'll get no complaints from me. I love the feeling of his cock inside me. It's just big and thick enough to make any girl moan, and moan I did when he's fully seated inside me. He struggles to stay still inside me, wanting me to acclimate to having such a large cock inside me but dying to get the show on the road.

The Devil groaned at how wet and warm my pussy was. I always come so hard and so intensely when it involves him. He rests his head momentarily on my shoulder. Fuck, did he feel amazing. The Devil leans down to nibble my left ear, his breath hot on my skin as he whispers to me.

"I was the one that gave you that orgasm. You screamed my name, pet, and I'll make you scream it again. This isn't going to be slow and gentle."

"Who said I wanted slow and gentle?"

"Wrap your legs around my waist."

I would be crazy not to do just that. Boy, did it feel amazing. I used my feet to dig into his ass, to drive him to push deeper, faster into me. The difference in angle and depth, wow. I was moaning and writhing under him as he fought desperately not to come just yet. He kept up a fast and unrelenting pace. He was so close now. I knew all of his facial expression so damn well.

"Who do you belong to?" he growls.

No reply. I bite back a smirk I so desperately want to give him.

"Don't get cheeky with me? Who. Do. You. Belong. To?" he accentuates each word with a thrust.

"Mmm… ah…. Y..you… the Ddd-evvil You."

"Good girl."

"Who makes you cum every time?"

"Y-yyy-ou do my Dddevil."

"Good girl. You want to cum?"

"Yes please."

"Asking permission for a woman like you. That's gold. Hold it."

"But-."

"I said hold it!"

"Mm."

Damn that man. He knows just how desperately I want to come. But I had to be a good girl and hold it. My body was straining to come. He damn well knew I couldn't hold out much longer. This was the holiday season. I'm expecting him to be a little charitable here.

"Come for me but scream my name so that every demon within 15 blocks knows who you belong to."

I smile at his command. I would never ever submit to any other being but him. I came hard, screaming his name until my voice was hoarse. My breathing was as ragged as the Devil's. He came soon after me, shouting my name.

He kissed me passionately, literally taking my breath away before he slowly slipped out of me, carefully lying next to me. He snaps his fingers and we're all cleaned up, simple as that. He motions for me to snuggle him. I smile and kiss all the way up his arm until I reached his face. The Devil grabs my waist and holds me possessively to him as we kiss.

We stop abruptly when the music changes to caroling. I look sheepishly back at him who looks more amused than anything else.

"Trying to get in the Christmas spirit, are we?"

"Hilarious. What if I was? You and your wicked games, darling. I'll have you know, it's all your fault. The rule of your little games is no death to your kin. So, I had to get creative. Apparently, the whole, 'Don't kill my demons' thing is more of a guideline since I did kill a couple outside just now."

"Always good to see if you can handle yourself. I worry about you out there. Nice to know you still have the moves."

"Another test? How romantic. Back to your original question I was pretending to be part of a caroling group."

The Devil laughs a hearty laugh.

"Clever girl. Good singing voice. I thought I heard you caroling outside."

"It's nice to know you can pick out my voice from six other people."

"Darlin' take the compliment."

Lilith chose to smile instead and reached over to shut off her phone.

"Are you staying for breakfast?" the Devil asks although he already knew the answer. Like I would book a job. He has me for the whole rest of the month. I have no more jobs aside from jobs in Hell. I'm all his.

"Of course. You've got me for the whole month at least. Unless you have pressing matters in Hell to at-."

"Hell can wait. I suggest you get some rest you'll need it."

I smile into the Devil's chest as sleep finally overtakes me. This was one hell of a holiday celebration. Can't wait to see what tomorrow has in store.

FOURTEEN

Mates *erotica*

Cayla growled in frustration and fell onto the bed right into her black satin pillow. "Argh!"

Dating was infuriating as a human but as a vampire, it had reached epic proportions. Lifting her head from her pillow she groaned at the sight around her. "Trashed" didn't even begin to cover the devastation. Honestly, it looked like she'd been robbed.

Just at that moment her bestie, Ellie, called to check in with her. Cayla answered the phone with a sigh.

"Trashed your bedroom, huh?"

"How do you always know?"

"Avoidance tactics. You're famous for them. You're going to be late! Put something on."

"Yeah, if it were that easy, the room wouldn't look this bad. My clothes are everywhere. Nothing fits; it's either too baggy, not the right color or too tight. Can vampires gain weight? Did I gain weight? What color goes with a first date? Well no, it's not *really* a first date. Isn't red a good color, don't guys gravitate towards red? But since we're vampires that's a bit on point isn't it?"

"Wow, well, I am *glad* I called?"

"Was that sarcasm?"

"This is a phone call not a text - you can hear my tone and no, no sarcasm intended. Get hold of yourself. You're going into a frantic monologue about clothes. Do I need to come over?"

"So, you're not mocking me."

"You saw how I was when I went on a first date with Mike. Oh my god, I was a mess. No mocking here. Now, for fashion advice, I suggest the black lace peplum dress. The very same one you stuffed in the back of the closet to only wear on special occasions. Girl, I'm serious, you wear those leather boots and we've got ourselves a special occasion."

"Why that one?"

"That's the only one still in the closet, right?"

"Seriously are you here? How do you know that?"

"I know you, silly girl. Put that on, trust me. You'll feel confident and powerful in that dress. You'll own it and that's what you need here. You need to feel like you've got this, like you're the awesome badass you are. You go get 'em girl. They won't know what hit 'em."

Cayla chuckled at Ellie. "Love you to death, girl."

"Cheeky you! We met at our deaths. Been friends how long now? Mmmm…a hundred years? Long enough girl, get some. Do not come back empty-handed, I'm serious. I will text you to check."

"Thanks for the fashion advice."

"Anytime girl. You got this. Mwah. Love ya"

"Mwah. Love ya."

Cayla sighed. She always felt better talking to Ellie. It almost made everything better. *Almost.* Well, until Cayla remembered the invitation she got two hours earlier for yet another wedding.

The stupid invitation was taunting her as it stuck out from the pile of clothes by the closet. She wished she had buried it better and all that it represented. Cayla really didn't see what was so bad about being single in the city. So what? She wasn't saddled with kids or some guy she couldn't stand; she was free to do whatever she wanted. The word "unmated" shouldn't be said with such disgust, only whispered in hushed sympathetic tones like it was a sickness. Please, she hadn't met *the right guy* and she refused to settle with *some guy*. Ellie got it and always managed to put the gossipers in their vampire clan to shame. But at times like these, alone in her apartment stressing about meeting men, the old conversations and digs came back to her. What's so good about being marked and mated? A slave to your mate? Feeling their feelings, hearing their thoughts? Hello ... can we say invasion of privacy. Creepy much. All she wanted was a good man who could love her for herself and she'd wait an eternity for it. Hell, she kind of already had.

Contrary to popular belief being single doesn't mean that Cayla was ugly or frumpy, quite the contrary. She was a vibrant, bubbly, badass vamp and the way she did her makeup only backed that up. She looked amazing, amazing enough to silence all those negative thoughts. Fuck her close-minded vampire clan mates. Maybe she'd find a mate or even her True Mate at this event and rub it in their faces. And maybe if she were lucky, he'd be smoking hot. A girl can dream. And dream she might have to because so far, the choices from every single vampire event were absolutely horrible, mind numbingly so. No wonder those vamps were single.

The ones she met online at Vampire Elite Matchmaker -- elite my ass -- were all hot, horny and ready to mate. And let's not mention the amount of dick pics poor Cayla had received or the one-liners, "Hey, you're hot and unmated. How about it?" Yeah, why bother to communicate and actually read people's profiles? So passé. What happened to dating? When did it become dick pics and random sex? It's not like vampires are pressed for time. They're not dying again, they have eternity to get it right. Cayla glanced at her vibrator on her way out. The night would probably end there anyway.

Cayla finally left her quaint little apartment near the woods, one of the few apartments on the outskirts of town. She wrapped her favorite slate blue scarf around her neck and started the long walk into town.

About thirty minutes later -- yes, her apartment was that far away -- she walked up to the unmarked building and was greeted instantly by an overly chipper woman with a clipboard. "Welcome to our first ever Vampire Speed Dating event. Yay! I hope everyone here leaves with a mate. What's your name?"

Cayla looked at her askance. *How is anyone that happy at meeting a stranger?* "Cayla Cartwright."

The woman didn't seem to notice Cayla's distain and focused instead on the paper in front of her. "Oh yes, I see you here. Welcome, Cayla. They're starting real soon. I know you'll find an amazing mate. Good luck, sweetie."

Cayla forced a smile, not sure the woman could deliver. Her usual vampire dates were never anything to brag about but at least Ellie had helped her pick out an awesome outfit. Cayla plopped down in a random seat in the back. *"Well, at least the chairs are comfy,"* she said to herself. The second Cayla saw a waiter, she flagged him down, "I'd like a screwdriver please." There was no need to do this sober.

In a matter of seconds, a bubbly sprite, a little slip of a thing dove out and energetically announced the start of the Vampire Speed Dating event that went by the name of, "Love at First Bite." *Yeah, not kidding you.* They choose that tacky title, thinking it fit well with the mood.

"Hello everyone, you'll have five minutes with each potential date. Put your best foot forward guys and gals and let's find love at first bite."

Cayla suppressed the need to retch at the catchphrase. She was just looking forward to getting this over with and forced herself not to roll her eyes. *"And so, it begins,"* she thought. *I'm going to have to nick-name people, so I remember them. I'm not going to remember five random names.* She looked down at the paper they provided to note which man she liked the best. *This agency was sure hopeful.*

Her first date was a real winner. *Cue the sarcasm.* He slowly sat down as if he were god's gifts to vampires. He smoothed down his silky shirt that was unbuttoned just a little to show an ample amount of chest hair. Actually, he looked more like a werewolf. Men usually don't flaunt that much chest hair. The man tousled his dark brown hair and wiggled his eyebrows. *Yeah, who needs speech when you can just try and eye fuck a stranger? Good job.* Then as if that wasn't bad enough, he smiled widely showing off bloody teeth. *What the hell dude? He seriously came here after butchering a human? There's no way with that much caked up blood, that the human survived. He's trying to sell me on a conquering warrior image? Try psychotic killer, dude. Seriously, what's the message here? I'm getting rampant amount of douche for sure. How is killing a human sexy or something to be proud of? I happen to be a vegan and not a murderer! And I definitely will not be dating any murderers.* Cayla recoiled from him in disgust, but he thought it was from fear. *Dumbass. Ok, I'm calling him Mr. Creepy Murder Guy.*

He spoke to her in a calm, gentle voice so as not to spook her anymore. "Hey, little one, it's okay."

I bet you're the one that's little, bucko. "It most assuredly is *not* OK," Cayla said confidently.

That was definitely not the answer he expected. He thought her bravery was just a front for her fear, so he continued to assuage her. *His idiocy knows no bounds.*

"No need to be afraid of me. I won't harm you. I know the blood on my teeth looks scary, but I was just hungry. I just came from dinner."

Cayla shivered at his words. *Came from dinner? Is he kidding?* He realized rather quickly that it was revulsion and not fear. The words she uttered next, made that quite clear. "Good to know that you flaunt your kills so brazenly. Heaven forbid a vampire actually thinks of humans as more than food, as precious things to be protected. We can choose to not be the monsters they think we are. We can choose to go vegan --."

The vampire in front of her was growing more upset as she went on. He decided he had had enough of her views on his life. He felt it wasn't her place to question his male wisdom. *Yeah, a real prize, this one.* He covered his anger well. His tone was mocking, thinking erroneously that he could wear her down and make her submit to his maleness. Ha!

He actually laughed and cut her off from saying anything else. *Rude, idiotic, macho and a murderer, wonderful. And that's why you're still single.*

"You're adorable really but you're a vampire, Cayla is it? Maybe you're a young one and you don't know what our kind does, but we don't make friends with humans. We eat them. Embrace it.

Embrace the inner monster. It's not something to be caged, it's something to be proud of. We are the superior beings."

"Pig's blood is fine with me."

He scoffed at her comment. "Pig's blood just doesn't have the same kick to it, does it? Nothing seasons blood like fear. Human blood makes you strong. But don't worry about that, when you're with me, I'll make sure you get big and strong off *real* blood."

"Cruelty is sexy now? You thought I would lie prostrate at your feet because you displayed that you're a killer. Because you have a dick? Please. Look bucko. No, I'm don't care what your real name is. Better I don't know. I am strong enough to kick your ass and as the rules state, any female can slap any male who is out of line. If you're not careful, you'll get more than a slap. I'll kill you or die trying. I'm a force to be reckoned with, not tamed or controlled.

Clearly, he was expecting a much more pliant and murderous mate. "I think you should keep looking," Cayla stated proudly and that made him really angry. His eyes were alight with a dangerous, murderous glint. Yep, this was going as well as she thought it would. Cayla sighed bored with his anger.

"I have never been insulted like -."

"Good, now you've learned, not all women like to be controlled. Move on."

Finally, the bell sounded. *Fucking finally.* All the men started to move to the next seat. The man in front of her clearly wanted to exchange more words but he was getting shoved by the next vampire. Mr. Creepy Murder Guy did proceed to let out a couple of growls to which Cayla sighed heavily and yawned at. *That was the longest, creepiest, sort of date of my life. Man, I hope this one is better.*

She turned her attention to her next suitor and shook his hand. Polite this one. *Off to a good start.*

"Hi. I'm Steve. Uh. You're like so awesome. I'm like…uh…this is so awesome…. Oh man I'm nervous. Can you tell I'm nervous, probably…uh but yeah….so…uh…hi?"

"Hi Steve."

Oh man is this gonna be awkward. Mr. Shy But Nice. I'll call him that.

He let out a nervous chuckle before he went into a monologue at rapid speed like he was being chased by someone. "Uh…ok so I like live with roommates in the center of town and I work as a customer service rep. So happy with that job. I get to work with people. I like humans, you know…like they're awesome. Got so much stuff workin' for 'em. And uh yeah, I'm happy with my job. Upper management looks scary."

Cayla worked to keep her face neutral. *Fuck is this guy boring. Nice, sweet but there's no passion, no chemistry. And he's giving me his life story from the get-go. Dude, really? I don't care. Wow me, don't bore me. He'd make a good husband for someone but not me.*

"So, what do you do?" he asked. *Whew! I can divert things to myself. Sort of better.*

"I'm a writer for the Vampire Daily."

"Get out. Oh my god, that's so awesome. Wow. A career woman. Wow. I can be the stay at home dad."

Really? Wow! So not something you say on a speed dating event. Maybe after date 3. Dating etiquette, dude.

The gong went off just at this moment and Cayla couldn't be happier. Cayla was polite as always and shook his hand telling him it was nice to meet him. It wasn't but there no need to be mean now.

The next man couldn't stop looking at her body. *Get a good look loser. Cause you're not getting this. This body is something you have to work for and someone like you wouldn't be able to put in the time. Sucks for you.* Cayla was content to stay silent. *If my date can't manage to speak why should I? He's the man, he should be taking the initiative. Hello, duh! I'll make an effort when he does.* Then shit got awkward because he started leering. From looking to leering to salivating. *Ew! Yeah, because speed dating equals a quick lay, right? If he's my soulmate, my True Mate, sure but a one-night stand from a speed dating event? Is he crazy?*

"You're unmated…perfect," he growled.

Cayla raised her eyebrows and gave him a glare.

"I believe this is the part where you're supposed to impress me."

"I'm nine inches and thick. Impressed yet?"

"Not really, so is my vibrator."

The look he gave to that answer was priceless. Cayla sucked down the remaining bits of her alcoholic drink all the while giving him stink eye. He looked down at her drink in disgust. He quickly flagged a waitress who he ogled as well. *How charming. Equal opportunity creep.*

"That drink is too ladylike and not strong enough for a woman that dates *my* kind. Get her something stronger, how about a whiskey on the rocks. No frilly, girly drinks."

His kind? What kind is that? I'm a vampire too and I don't kowtow.

"Excuse me. I can't order for myself?" Cayla yelled incredulously.

"Not if you order that."

"Wow! No wonder you're single." Cayla replied with disdain. She then grabbed a drink off the waitress's tray and shoved it in his face. He yelled something about a damaged shirt, but Cayla could care less. In a second, she was in the restroom. If she didn't duck in there, she would have definitely punched him. She only exited the restroom when the bell rang again.

When Cayla came back to the table, "Mr. Nine Inches," moved to the next table but not before giving her a hurt look.

"If his ego is as big as his cock, he'll get over it. The girl next to me looks willing. She'll stroke it for him. Good luck to the both of them."

"My, my what do we have here? In that dress? This late at night? Unmated? We could mate quickly. For your protection," the man said hopefully.

Oh my god if someone else says the word unmated, I will strangle them. I have standards, people, which no one is living up to mind you. How hard is to find a decent guy?! I don't want a quick fuck! But can I say all that? No! Then I'll seem like a bitch. I have to be polite. And I can protect myself dammit!

"I can handle myself," Cayla replied with scorn.

The vampire in front of her quickly backtracking shaking his head vigorously. "I'm sorry, I-I'm new to all of this. Turned rather recently. All these changes are hard you know, and I haven't-uh-haven't mated yet with anyone. You're beautiful and tough and you know what you want. It's so invigorating. I would love the chance to know you if you'd let me."

Now that was unexpected. Another nice guy but I'm 100 years old. I'd have to teach him everything! How to kiss, how to feed properly, how to have sex, guard him against bloodlust, everything and he looked like a kid. It's too much. I don't want to have to show someone how to be the man I want, I don't want to change anyone, nor do I have the patience to teach men. I want a guy that makes me weak in the knees the second I see him. A man who knows what he wants and how to make me beg for it. I could be happy with this one, if only I had the patience to be his teacher.

"Look, Brian, is it?"

"Yes miss."

Miss? That's very sweet, too sweet. No rough edges to be sure. Mr. Good Guy.

"You're very sweet and you'd make a great mate but I'm looking for my True Mate here. Been waiting a long time. 100 years actually. What's a few more at this point."

The man smiled a genuine smile. "I wish you were my True Mate."

Cayla gave him a genuine smile back. "I hope you find yours here," she offered.

"The only two people looking for a True Mate and it isn't us."

"Yeah, that's totally my luck."

"Well, Cayla it was lovely to have the chance to talk to you. I wish you the best."

"It was lovely talking to you too, Brian. I hope you find the one."

Cayla had a mind to leave but thankfully there was only one more date. She'd be leaving soon enough. Cayla promised Ellie that she would stick this out until the end, give it a real shot. The last man wasn't bad, he was very nice. Not confidant with a rough edge like she wanted but a man she could be happy with. The fact that he wasn't her True Mate reminded her just how lonely she was.

The bell sounded, and the next man appeared. She wasn't prepared for what happened next. Cayla was expecting a date on par with the others, but this wasn't like any other date.

It was as if time froze, the people around her disappeared and so did the whole event. It was as if they were the only two people there.

The man slowly turned in her direction and her heart stopped. He was wearing a leather jacket and a faded band tee of an obscure indie rock band she couldn't believe he'd heard of much less liked. His shirt was stretched taunt over his substantial muscles. His tight black jeans left nothing to the imagination. Let's just say he was big all over. He walked with purpose and commanded the room but was looking only at her.

He was hands down the single most attractive man she had ever seen, and he was smiling at her. Cayla wanted to thank the universe for putting this man in her path. A man that looked like a male model but edgier, more like a guy from the cover of a bodice ripper.

Is it hot in here or is it just him? There is no way that he's my destined mate. I mean hey, I'm hot as all get out but I'm not stick skinny. I eat, you know, and I don't necessarily watch what I eat. I have curves that define me but curves none the less. And I'm a klutz, like a major klutz and I'm overly emotional and I stress over stupid stuff. I get impulsive sometimes, I can snap at people. I'm not perfect. A man like that needs "perfect" -- not me. Maybe he's looking at someone behind me? Huh? There's just a plant behind me. Okay maybe he is looking at me? His gaze is so intense. He's devouring me with his eyes. And they're so goddamn blue. I feel like I'm drowning in the ocean here. I could look at them forever.

The vampire seemed to take forever to reach his seat. The seconds seemed to stretch out ad infinitum until finally he stood behind the seat he was meant to sit in and smiled at her, his hands running up and down the back of his chair. The smile he offered her told volumes, the perfect promise of sweet with a just a hint of a rough night ahead. For this man, Cayla would break her "no sex on the first date" rule. Hell, who wouldn't for this guy? This man looked like he knew how to please. Cayla hoped she got the chance to sample his wares, so to speak. He slowly pulled his chair out and sat down. This vampire definitely knew exactly what effect he had on women and he was enjoying it. *Damn him.*

When he sat down, Cayla was assaulted with his scent. *How is it possible that he not only looks that hot, but smells absolutely divine? Damn it, did I just gasp? People are looking at me funny. Wait -- how does he smell like the cherry pie my mom baked me every day after school, blended with the woods behind my house during a rainstorm? That's a specific smell. I cannot moan out loud! That would be creepy. Yeah, he's hot and fuck does he smell good but rein it in girl. We don't want to inflate his ego too much now. Play it cool.*

The man chuckled, amused with Cayla's silence and, though she didn't remember this detail at the moment, True Mates can read the minds of their beloved.

I find you equally pleasing darling. You smell like a hilltop of fresh roses and you look amazing. I can't believe you're single. As much as I would love to keep listening to your running commentary, which is quite amusing, I do think we should talk a bit lest the others ask uncomfortable questions, or the bell goes off. And yes, I'm saying this in your mind. We are True Mates.

He chuckled at her lost look. She wasn't expecting to actually find her True Mate here or have him look like this? He leaned over, anxious to shake her hand and find out more about her. The second their hands touched a warmth flooded their bodies. And their forearms seemed to glow like there was a light under their skin. He held Cayla's hand and saw a tattoo form instantly on her wrist as if someone were writing his name in calligraphy there. She turned over his wrist and saw her name written there. The vampire leaned in and smelled her, his nose in her hair. The shampoo she used was delicious, the perfect blend of citrus and lilacs and her scent was mouthwatering. He quickly let go of her hand.

"I'm Vincent," he said confidently in direct opposition to how flustered he looked; cheeks flushed, breathing ragged, hands white knuckling the table.

"Cayla," she said reverently. *His scent is driving me crazy. So, this is what they all felt? This connection? Well, now I understand the hype, I really do.*

After all the smoothness Vincent had, he seemed slightly nervous now and an awkward silence fell over the conversation. I mean what is there to say after you realize you're soulmates and you have all eternity to get to know one another and fall in love. Asking what music, you like or what's your favorite color kind of sounds ridiculous in that light.

So they simply stared at each other, amazed that they had found one another. Vincent reached over and took Cayla's hand. "How about we get out of here?" His tone wasn't sexual but instead sincere. He looked at her, amazed that she was his.

Cayla beamed at him and gladly took his hand. The bell went off and the bubbly woman came back probably to make an announcement about how to specify your preference but in this case, that was a non-issue.

She instantly saw the two of them attempting to walk out holding hands. She gasped and ran over to them forgetting all about her announcement.

"No. No. That's not how it works. You have to -."

Vincent proudly held up his right wrist. The only exception to any rule was the True Mate clause. He then proceeded to hold Cayla tight, his arm winding around her possessively. Cayla should have been a bit taken aback but this was her soulmate after all. His touch felt comforting. And she liked the possessiveness. This model was all hers; he could get as handsy as he wanted. She was sure he could back it up.

The woman stared at Cayla, for the first time really looking at her. Her brows wrinkled as she looked at both of them and then a scowl formed on her face. Vincent simply turned to Cayla and nodded at her as they both walked out without saying anything to anyone. Cayla finally realized what was so special about this connection. She understood why her friends were hounding her to find "the one."

Right on cue, Ellie texted. "Are you going home solo or with some guy? Anyone decent?"

"Actually, I found my True Mate. I promise to call tomorrow."

"WHAT?! OMG! Girl, seriously? What? How does he look? What is he like? What does he like? What's his name? How old is he? OMG! Can I call you?"

"Tomorrow. I promise."

"You better girl. This is huge. OMG you owe me for pushing you to go. You're welcome girl. Go get some and tell me EVERY-THING! You know what I mean, when you wake up. Mwah."

Cayla chuckled as she put her phone away. "Sorry, that was my bestie. She demanded a full report. I just gave her an outline."

Vincent smiled back at her. "That's okay, I was texting my best friend as well."

He reached over and grabbed her hand and they walked in silence for a bit just enjoying being together at night in the city. They walked aimlessly around the city talking, eating ice cream, drinking coffee and just catching up on all the centuries they'd been alive. She found out that over his lifetime, he had done almost every job imaginable. He found out that she always chose a job doing something artistic. They bonded over music and movies. They even ran into a midnight showing of an indie horror flick. They laughed and gasped at exactly the same moments. Horror movies always got monsters wrong and especially vampires. His arm was around her holding her tight the entire time. It was the perfect date. After all this time it felt so good to feel like she belonged with someone. It felt good to have someone hold her.

And of course, neither one wanted the date to end. It was going so well that Cayla decided to take him home. She totally forgot about the mess in her room and as they entered her room kissing passionately, might I add, they didn't notice their surroundings. His hands were firmly on her waist pulling her towards him. Her arms were around his neck, grabbing onto his hair to deepen the kiss. And in one fell swoop they both fell into a giant pile, nearly burying themselves in clothes.

"Um. Oh shit. I totally forgot. I'm not usually this messy. I just couldn't decide what to wear and-."

Vincent laughed such a hearty laugh before reaching for her over all the clothes. "I'm glad you chose the dress. Good choice," he offered hoping to allay her concerns. "Really, it's okay. You should have seen my roommate 50 years ago. This is neat compared to him."

"Do you have a picture for confirmation?"

Vincent grabbed her hand and sent her a mental picture. "That *is* worse. Thanks for the proof."

Vincent chuckled at her, finding her absolutely adorable.

Vincent noticed that Cayla was as nervous as he was. She was biting her lip and looking around the room. There was a connection here, but they had only known each other for a few hours. Vincent tried to assuage his mate. *We're True Mates. We're connected. We don't have to have sex, we could just sleep next to each other. There's no rush. We have eternity. I can feel you're nervous. Whatever you want is okay. No pressure.*

I am nervous, but I want to do this. You're my True Mate, it's going to be awesome. Why wait? I'd like to see what you can do.

Oh, I can do a lot.

Put your money where your mouth is, big boy.

How do you know I'm big?

Your pants leave nothing to the imagination.

So you've been looking?

As if you haven't been looking at me?

Touché my darling. Vincent smirked at Cayla and wiggled his eyebrows. On him, it was adorable.

Vincent slowly, gently kissed Cayla. She leaned into it as he deepened the kiss, holding onto to her hair. Vincent felt surer of himself now and grabbed her hips possessively bringing her closer to him. He nibbled on her neck and collarbone making her moan. He smiled against her neck. He loved hearing that sound.

Wanting to get the show on the road, he slowly moved his hands down to Cayla's back to take off her dress. Everything was going great when suddenly the zipper caught halfway down. Vincent unzipped and zipped the dress thinking that would fix the problem but as luck would have it, another problem surfaced. Once the dress was almost off, after several minutes of fighting with said zipper, he had to contend with a small button to take the dress completely off. The button proved to be quite a difficult foe only to fly right into Vincent's eye.

Cayla took the moment to shed the dress completely off, throwing the offending dress off into a pile in the corner.

"Ow. Got me in the eye that time. That should really come with a warning label."

"I'm glad I'm not the only klutz here."

"Your true soulmate."

They both chuckled at that.

"Should we brave onward?"

"I can take it. Bring on the buttons," Vincent said with bravado.

Cayla giggled and wasted no time. She wadded through the piles of messy clothes and inched closer to him to tear off his shirt. She managed to unbutton his shirt in seconds and then moved to take it off his head, but it got stuck mid-way. She pulled even harder and pushed Vincent into the wall by mistake.

"Stop moving there, darling. Come on, sit on the bed. I think I've got this. I'm refusing to let your shirt win. That's it. It's coming off!" Cayla said confidently.

In a couple of seconds, Cayla had the shirt off, no problem. Vincent being a good sport and an easy-going guy, threw his hands up in triumph. "We survived Act Two!"

Cayla laughed. "That we did."

Vincent held up his hand and they high-fived. Cayla never thought sex with this male model would be like this, but this was what she needed. A carefree, funny guy who could lighten up anything. And he was just as klutzy as she was, perfect.

"I'll have you know that sex on the first date is not my forte, but we are True Mates after all. Our first time together is going to be an adventure and I wouldn't want it any other way."

Vincent chuckled rather enjoying her view of things. "I'm one lucky guy to snag you."

"I feel the same way about you. So next up is your pants, big boy. Let's do it."

Vincent nodded and unzipped his pants halfway when he cut his penis. Shit. He actually caught his penis on a zipper. What? He had boxers on. He groaned and placed his hand over his cock as he gently pulled the zipper the rest of the way down. He pulled back a little rocking his hips to try and shake the fabric the rest of the way down. He then took down his boxers. Once he did, he cupped his penis and looked at it. Only a small cut.

Cayla bit her lip to suppress a giggle as she looked over at him. Vincent walked over to her but toppled over before he got to her, his pants and boxers wound around his ankles.

"You okay down there? Little Vincent okay too?"

"My fall was cushioned by your clothes."

"I'm glad my clothes could be of assistance."

"Oh, nice top by the way."

"Hey, that's my favorite top actually."

"And Little Vincent is fine, it's just a small cut. And he's not very little is he?"

"Boy, you are klutzy. He's big for penises but small in reference to all of you."

"You might have to make it up to Little Vincent later."

"I'd be happy to," Cayla replied with a wink.

From the floor, Vincent took his pants the rest of the way off along with his boxers. He slowly stood up and when he did, he found Cayla naked.

"I know. Our first time should be sensual, and we should undress each other but judging by how our clothes are faring, I thought it prudent to save my bra and undies the rough treatment. But in round two, I can put them back on. They were lace."

"I love a woman in lace. Quite right. Wouldn't want them to get destroyed. Round 2 I like the sound of that."

"Protection?" Cayla asked. Vampires couldn't have children, except if they were True Mates. And Vampires weren't susceptible to most venereal diseases, but they could have a few nasty ones. Better safe than sorry.

"Protection against me?"

Cayla actually giggled. "Oh man, that I needed. Your klutziness is not dangerous to me, clothes maybe. No silly. Protection. A raincoat, a condom. Do you have one?"

"Ohhh yeah, hold on?"

Vincent bent down and dug into his pockets for a condom, finding two. He grabbed one and smiled at her holding it up, proud of himself somehow. He then tried to open it. He tried one end and then the other. It wouldn't give. He tried again. Still nothing. What the hell? He then tried to tear it with his teeth. That was a no go and now the package was wet. He tried again really using all of his strength this time but only managed to make himself unbalanced and fell over yet again. He quickly brushed himself off and tried one last time. He managed to open it, but he tore the condom in the process. It went flying through the air and stuck onto the wall on the other side of the room.

Cayla turned, impressed that he was not only this klutzy but that he had such impressive aim. This hot guy was totally her soulmate, no question about it.

"I'll try the other one. Uh that one got stuck to the wall," he said sheepishly.

Cayla fought to keep her face bland. Vincent took a deep breath willing it to open. This one opened without any problems.

Vincent sighed happily as he placed the condom on his throbbing cock, feeling very proud of himself. Cayla pushed him down and straddled him. He made like he was going to protest but she put a finger on his lips.

"With the luck we're having, me on top may be the best choice. Besides, I already know what I like and judging by that huge cock, I know you can satisfy. You can show me what you got round 2 big boy, deal?"

Vincent smirked at her. She was one hell of a woman.

Cayla slowly sank down on his cock. She was already wet through the whole ordeal. Anyone looking at that hot specimen of a man would be regardless of the slight setbacks. Vincent was bigger than any of her boyfriends and stretched her walls deliciously. She felt so full with him inside her. Cayla groaned before she started to move slowly at first to get used to his girth inside her and to see which angles really worked for her. When she mapped it all she sped up spiraling towards her orgasm and bringing Vincent along for the ride. She relished the --feel of his cock suddenly filling her up to the brim and then sliding out of her.

"You feel fucking amazing. You're huge and -."

"Sweetheart you feel amazing too, tightest, warmest pussy ever. You're mine. All mine."

"Only if you're mine."

"You know I am."

Cayla could hear Vincent moaning and writhing under her. She really enjoyed seeing him like that knowing that she was the cause.

Cayla leaned back as she rode Vincent's hard cock. She touched her own breasts kneading them softly in her hands. She moaned and gasped with each tug on her nipple. Vincent watched her with rapt interest memorizing what she liked.

Vincent growled enjoying the show but needed desperately to have contact with her, to kiss those luscious lips. He made a grabby gesture motioning Cayla to come down, so he could kiss her. She obliged and kissed him passionately grabbing his hair and fisting her hands in it.

The new position was amazing, and she moaned even louder this time. His arm wound around, and held her waist down as his hips pushed his cock up inside her. He kept an inhumanely fast pace. She was screaming his name and he was growling hers. Cayla's head was down on his shoulder, her teeth nibbling the skin there. She was so close but tried to hold on.

"Close… Viincent…I…mmmm?" Cayla wasn't sure whether she was asking permission to come or whether she was warning him. Her brain couldn't think about anything but the immense pleasure he was giving her.

He licked his lips and tried to think. She wanted him to answer something but what was the question again? "Mmm…hmm…yes?"

And that was all the encouragement she needed. Cayla bit down on his neck just as Vincent bit down on hers. Their orgasms crashed through them at the exact same time. They greedily lapped up the blood and reverently said each other's names. Cayla's licked the wound on Vincent's neck, sure that it would be quite a prominent mating mark. Vincent looked at his handiwork on Cayla's neck and was sure of the same thing. They stayed inside each other, chests heaving, blissed out, their blood coursing through them binding them as mates forever. Cayla put her head down on Vincent's chest and just lay there enjoying the afterglow and their connection through the bond. Cayla had never had a more intense orgasm. Vincent chuckled happily before they slowly extricated themselves. Cayla could get used to those orgasm and this wonderful man as her mate.

Vincent went to the bathroom to clean up and proceeded to knock over everything in there at least twice. Cayla laughed, and

Vincent closed his eyes. He loved hearing her laugh. He smiled at his own reflection. *"She's all mine. That amazing woman is mine and for once, she's not scared of my klutzy nature -- she finds it endearing and similar to hers. She's an amazing woman and she's mine."*

"You know I can hear you. Get out of that bathroom before you break something and hand me that towel," Cayla stated in an uneven voice as she fought the urge to laugh.

Vincent blushed forgetting about the telepathy for a second before he ran out to clean her up, using vampire speed. "I'm just as happy to have you as my True Mate. My hot, klutzy, adorable, sweet vampire mate. You're perfect, Vincent."

"And so are you," he said as he placed a kiss on her forehead.

In a matter of seconds, they were clean and fast asleep, Cayla snuggled into Vincent's chest. Even vampires needed rest and after mating and bonding, they needed it even more. They both fell asleep with smiles on their face, content and happy that they had finally found each other.

Who would have guessed that they would find true love at a Vampire Speed Dating event? Cayla owed Ellie for pushing her to go. She was so grateful she went, and she couldn't wait to spend eternity with Vincent. She was one lucky girl.

———————————

About the Author

Lexie Carver is a feisty woman who lives out loud, a veritable badass. Lexie has been writing since she was a child; she's always loved horror and making people scared. Most of her stories come from her very vivid dreams. She always wakes up to at least one cup of black coffee and loves listening to indie rock.

Lexie Carver

Visit www.lexiecarver.com

Email: lexiecarver69@gmail.com
Twitter: Lexie_Carver
Tumblr: @roxy-davenport
Facebook: www.facebook.com/lexiecarverthehorrorwriter
Spotify: Lexie Carver

www.ingramcontent.com/pod-product-compliance
Lightning Source LLC
Chambersburg PA
CBHW020308150626
46552CB00022B/2080

* 9 7 8 0 6 9 2 1 7 9 5 7 4 *